SECRETS IN THE SHADOWS OF HOUSE NASSAU

BY

BRANDON SCRANTON

Published by Franklin Publishers
Printed in the United States of America

For permissions, inquiries, or additional copies, contact:
Franklin Publishers
www.franklinpublishers.com

Dedication

To my sister -

Not just family, but my best friend and co-warrior in life.

You have had no doubts in my abilities and always my cheerleader!

Acknowledgement

Kris Wall –

Thank you for taking the time out of your busy work schedule to help me with editing my book.

Greatly Appreciated!

Table of Contents

Chapter: 1...1

Chapter: 2...12

Chapter: 3...23

Chapter: 4...33

Chapter: 5...45

Chapter: 6...52

Chapter: 7...65

Chapter: 8...75

Chapter: 9...90

Chapter: 10...100

Chapter: 11...110

Chapter: 12...123

Chapter: 13...132

Chapter: 14...150

Chapter: 15...162

Chapter: 16...173

Chapter: 17..179

Chapter: 18..192

Chapter: 19..207

Author's Biography..214

Chapter

1

The late Earl Nassau died unexpectedly a month ago. His son, Robert, had inherited the title, Earl Nassau, and the ancestral home. Before his death, Earl Nassau had been the Minister of Defense for the Kingdom of the Netherlands. Robert had left home twenty years prior to go to law school in London and has not seen his father since.

Michael had never met his paternal grandfather, but was well-versed in his family history. As a sixteen-year-old, he was almost a carbon copy of his father, Robert. Tall, slender, dark hair, and dark eyes make Michael and his father appear more mysterious than they were.

For the past three weeks, Michael had been traveling in the Netherlands with his parents. Robert, and Michael's mother, Mary had been spending most of their free time with him as usual, but they had been working as they traveled.

His mother awoke Michael early. He and his parents had been staying at the Noordeinde Palace for the past two nights. Today was the first of June 1920, and it was the first day of many changes for Michael Nassau.

About an hour after Michael awoke, he found himself sitting between his parents inside their new motorcar, a Rolls Royce. The seats were much more comfortable than those of the train or the ship. They have spent the past week at Dam Palace in Amsterdam and at Noordeinde Palace in Den Haag. Michael and his parents have been in their new motorcar for most of their travels.

Their new driver was now taking them to House Nassau. It was called a house, but it was an actual palace. Their driver was one of several new staff members and only joined the family when they arrived. While riding to his ancestral home, Robert reads over several sheets of paper. Michael saw "House Nassau Staff" typed on the top of the page.

Michael's father reads off the new staff names to his son and wife. They were not moving any of the staff from their London home. Mary is the daughter of an English Earl, and they lived on the Royal Crescent with the staff provided by her father's estate. Michael had developed a friendship with the first footman and was sad to learn he would not join them in the Netherlands.

The Rolls-Royce turned off the road onto the long gravel drive to the ancestral home. Robert became physically uncomfortable, and Michael could see a look of apprehension on his father's face. This was not a day that Robert looked forward to, but he knew it would happen one day.

Farmland and animals lined the long drive. As the road curved to the left, Michael got his first sight of his new home. It was smaller than Dam Palace but is larger than Noordeinde Palace. He saw a majestic fountain on the main drive close to the entry. House Nassau was grander than he could imagine. The stone façade was imposing and unlike anything he had seen before. Expansive windows provided an unobstructed view lining all of the visible exterior walls.

The motorcar slowed to a stop between the grand entry and the large fountain. A statue of Prince William Oranje-Nassau stood in the center of the fountain. All of the house staff were lined up to greet the family. While the butler opened the left door to the Rolls-Royce for Mary, Robert climbs out of the right side. Michael followed his father out of the motorcar. All of the staff bowed to the family in sync. A man extended a hand to assist Mary out. "My lady, I am Lars, the butler." As Robert walked around, Lars bowed again. Robert reached out a hand and shook Lars' hand. "This is our son, Meneer Michael." Lars bowed a third time as Michael announces, "Pleasure to meet you."

Lars reminded Michael of the butler at their London home. He was wearing his formal black suit with a waistcoat and black tie. The high white collar looked uncomfortable to Michael. His dark black hair was parted perfectly to the left, and he appeared to be freshly shaven for this event. Slightly larger than his last butler, but Lars looked like any butler he had seen growing up.

As the three walked and greeted the other staff, Michael was still at a loss for words. This was much more formal than he was used to. Robert spoke to Michael about his Dutch heritage and about his late grandfather, but nothing prepared him for this. In London, they lived in a large home with staff, but nowhere near this level. His maternal grandparents' country estate looked miniature in comparison.

House Nassau was built in 1620, and it was a thirty-minute drive from The Hague. Robert's office is in The Hague inside of Parliament, so the location is ideal. They arrived at their new home about nine o'clock in the morning.

After meeting the staff, Mary took Michael's arm. "Your room is there," she said, pointing to four large windows over the main grand entrance. "Grab your luggage and go up," his father continued. "Your mother and I need to tend to a few things, then we will have lunch at noon." His father smiled and patted his son's shoulder.

Lars met them at the door, and with his Dutch accent, he asked Michael, "May I take your luggage, Meneer Michael?"

"I can handle them. Thank you," Michael replied quickly. Lars simply bowed to Michael and guided him inside.

Michael's parents went into the large formal room next to the entry, where several people were waiting. Lars escorted Michael to his new room on the first floor. Michael was looking around at the interior of his new home. Several large portraits of strangers, several chandeliers, and carpeting lined the steps and hallways. "If you need or want anything, just pull the bell cord" Lars stated. He continued with, "Your other luggage has been unpacked already." Michael thanked him and stood in the middle of the large room. Michael's old bedroom was not as large as his new one.

He placed his luggage onto the grand bed, as he could not stop looking at the new room. There is a large, tiled fireplace from floor to ceiling was one end, with the bed facing it. The walls were covered with dark wood; the ceilings were carved wood, and the windows had large shutters painted an amazing blue. Nothing in the room looked like it once belonged to his father. He took a deep breath and noted the smell. A smile came to the 16-year-old's face. "I like the smell of history," he thought. "I think it is a combination of an old wooden trunk, fresh linen, leather, and – yes – chocolate."

He walked around the large room, noting the amount of furniture in the room. Four large armchairs were next to the big windows. The bed was bigger than anything he had seen before, and several portraits of ships lined the walls. A couple of large antique wardrobes stood off to one side. A chest of drawers was between them. Several of his items had already been laid out on top of it.

A note on a bedside table caught his attention. It had his name on it and is folded in half. "Meneer Michael, I will be in your room after the evening meal to introduce myself. My name is Willem, and I will be your new teacher."

Michael sighed. He was attempting to come to terms with his new life and now a new teacher. Michael's father is the new private secretary to the Dutch Prime Minister. His paternal grandfather was the first cousin of Queen Wilhelmina of the Kingdom of the Netherlands. Michael had never met him, but understood the significance of his family history. This was the first time he had to face it, though.

Michael went to a private school in London with his best friend Charles. Charles was currently on holiday with his parents in Belgium. Now that Robert would be the Earl, Michael would be getting his education from a tutor at the palace.

The clock on the mantel now showed ten o'clock. The tall, gold gilded clock ticked softly and chimed on the hour. "What to do for two hours," Michael thought. He was close to his mother and father, and often sat nearby to them, even during official meetings. However, today felt different to him. He did not wish to be in the way, and did not know enough Dutch to understand everything anyhow. A knock at the door interrupted his thoughts.

A very tall man was standing on the other side. "Hallo, Meneer Michael. I am one of the footmen, and I have a note from your mother," he stated as he handed Michael a small note with his mother's handwriting on it. "Thank you," he replied as he took the note. Michael felt this footman looked similar to the one he had in London for a short time. He had not remembered that Antoon had been there helping them transition. Glancing at the note, he was delighted to read that his best friend would come to stay for the summer months. She wrote that Charles would arrive around eleven o'clock this morning.

The footman explained that the room next to his has been prepared for Lord Charles. "What is your name?" asked Michael. "I am Antoon, sir," the footman replied. "Nice to meet you, Antoon and thank you." Antoon smiled, "You must not remember me, sir, I was with you and your parents for the first week of your move." Michael blushed, "I am sorry, Antoon, I do not remember seeing you there." Antoon assured Michael that it was okay that he was not remembered. Michael felt embarrassed, but Antoon's quick reply calmed him. "It is my job not to be noticed, sir," as he turned and walked down the long hallway.

A few minutes passed, and Michael's father entered the room. Robert grew up in the estate, and this was his childhood bedroom. "How do you like the room?" Robert asked his son. "Smells like history," Michael responded, still thinking about how the old building smelled.

Robert walked over to the wall next to the grand fireplace. He spoke to himself, "I wonder if I can remember where it is," as he panned around the room. Robert pushed onto the paneling, revealing a secret door. Michael's jaw dropped. "Where does that go?" Michael asked, very excitedly. Robert turned to his son with a smile. "Many-many places." The two walked through the doorway, and Robert led the way.

Trekking along the hidden hallway and then down

a flight of stairs, they stood in front of another door. Michael was excited to see where their short journey had taken them. Robert took out a key and unlocked the door with a grin on his face, ushering Michael through. Michael found himself standing next to a grand fireplace in the study on the ground floor.

"I would often come down at night to see my father," Robert explained. The two sat down by the windows, which overlooked the large botanical gardens and the lake on the estate. The room's spaciousness, high-end finishes, ample natural light, and comfortable yet stylish furniture provided proof of the title Earl of Nassau. The family crest was engraved in almost everything that could be engraved.

"Michael, I want you to understand something. I did not have the type of relationship with my father that you and I have." Michael looked at his father and noticed an expression he had never seen on him before. "Why did I never meet your parents?" Michael continued, "I know mother's parents." Michael grew up spending time with his maternal grandparents only. "My father put his country before his own family," Robert explained. "In a few days' time, I will explain more, but I want you to know your mother and I want you to be happy and comfortable."

The study was lined with paintings, wood paneling, two beautiful chandeliers, and enough furniture to accommodate a large gathering. Robert pointed to the antique desk in the room's corner. "That desk is almost as old as the palace." Michael walked over and sat in the chair. Facing him was a photo of his parents and

Michael as a young child. "Where did this come from?" He picked it up and held it closer. Michael recognized the background as their home in London.

Robert stood next to his son and looked at the photo. "My father kept track of us, even though we had not spoken since I left for London." Michael replaced the photo and continued to examine the oversized desk. Robert placed a key into the left top drawer, unlocked it, and pulled it open. Inside, he pulled out a few papers with handwriting on them. "These are the letters my father left for me to read after his death. They were given to me with his will." Robert walked over to the fireplace while looking at them with some detail.

"Father, do you regret going to London?" Robert quickly turned around to face his son. "Not in the slightest," Robert looked up to the large painting of his father above the fireplace and sighed. "I will show you around a little. I must return to the library soon to rescue your mother from the staff."

Robert placed the letters back into the desk drawer and locked it. "These are duplicate keys to the study and my desk," Robert said as he handed Michael the keys. "I ask that you do not lose these. I am entrusting them to you." Michael quickly placed them in his trouser pocket. "I will not lose them, father." Robert gestured for Michael to follow him through the double doors out of the study. He continued to guide his son past the grand staircase and into a window-lined hallway. Michael saw several large windows and even more paintings.

"Who are all these men, father?" Robert stopped in front of the first painting. "This is the first Earl Nassau. Each one is an Earl, and each one is your family." Michael looked overwhelmed at this time. His father often spoke of the family history. "You will have a portrait in this hallway when you become the Earl Nassau," said Robert to his young son. Michael became pale with that thought of being the next Earl Nassau.

The two arrived at the far end of the heavily decorated hallway. Robert turned and looked at another painting of his father. "Here is my father in his military uniform." Michael stood next to his father to see the masculine male posing, looking down at them. "The Dutch aristocracy differs from the British one. There are a few titled families left here," Robert explained.

"This wing is the original portion of the house, and it was built in 1544 by Prince William van Oranje-Nassau." Michael could not help but notice he strongly resembled his father and grandfather. The estate has been added to little by little. Most of the estate was from 1620.

As Michael and his father continued to review family paintings, Robert explained why he left the Netherlands. "My father and I were never close. He always put this country before himself and his family. My younger brother, Noah, stayed here with our father during the Great War, and when your uncle was killed, which left my father here alone. My mother died from consumption when I was close to your age. I guess that is why I include you in everything."

As the two walked back towards Robert's study, Michael stopped in the middle of the grand hall. The young man was still trying to absorb the grand palace and what would be his future. Everything that Michael could see was much more than the young man could process. The original glass made a rainbow of colors on the walls and floors. Michael turned around to find his father watching him. His face held a look that Michael had never seen before. Robert had the look of what Michael interpreted as his father feeling overwhelmed.

Robert walked his son back to his study. "We are cousins to Her Majesty, but our family is not in line for the throne. We have an important role to perform, and I will make sure you are ready when it is your time." Robert continued, "We asked Charles' parents to allow him to spend the summer months here. I encourage you both to explore everything in the house and grounds."

The sound of a motorcar pulled up. "That must be Charles now," said Robert. Michael ran to the grand entrance to see the Nassau Rolls-Royce pull up. Robert opened the large main doors and followed his son outside. Charles got out before the driver even shut the vehicle off, much less get out to open Charles' door for him.

Chapter

2

Charles stepped out of the motorcar smiling widely. The two young men have always been best friends. Before Robert became the secretary to the Dutch Prime Minister, he was the personal solicitor for many influential people in London. Charles' father is a Duke and close friends with Robert and Mary. Michael's maternal grandfather is an Earl and introduced the families. Robert moved to London for university to study law almost twenty years ago, and that is where he met and married Mary.

The two young men greeted each other, and Michael asked, "How was your journey?"

"Great, I came by train from Belgium today. Mother and father will remain for a few more weeks," Charles explained. "How are you settling in?" asked Charles. Michael sighed heavily.

"We arrived only a couple of hours ago. We stayed in

Amsterdam and The Hague for a few days, then we were driven here today."

Charles has platinum blond hair with emerald-green eyes. His shirt had become untucked and looked as if he had not cared about getting dressed that morning – or any morning, truth be told. Michael and Charles are the complete opposites. Michael is the tall and reserved of the two friends, Charles is shorter, boisterous, and disheveled – looking, no matter the time of day or activity at hand. One could go as far as calling Michael shy and very self-aware. Still, they are the best of friends.

Lars and a footman collected the luggage and showed Charles to his room. The boys walked behind them, and Michael pointed to his own room as they walked by. "I have something to show you before lunch," Michael whispered.

Charles' room was like Michael's. "A passage connects the rooms," said Lars as he pointed to the narrow door. "This room belonged to Michael's Uncle Noah," he told the boys. Lars issued a reminder as he walked out, stating, "Do not forget the mid-day meal in the small dining room, Meneer Michael." Upon Michael's short nod in acknowledgment, Lars swiftly left the room.

"Uncle Noah," Michael thought. "I do not remember my uncle Noah," he said out loud. "He was killed in an accident during the Great War. Before the war, he lived here with grandfather."

"Sad," replied Charles. "I had several family members killed in the war, also."

Michael looked out the door and down the hall to make sure Lars was gone. He was excited to show his friend the secret door his father had showed him. "Wow!" Charles exclaimed as Michael opened the hidden door. "It is just like the mystery books," he continued. "Where does it go?" as Charles investigates the door. "Father said they go all over the estate. The servants used them to move around without being seen."

Michael took his friend along the same path that his father had taken him, which led to the study. "Excellent," Charles exclaimed with a cheeky smile. "We can explore more after we eat," replied Michael, also smiling widely. The duo began looking for the small dining room where lunch was being served.

They set off down the long hall lined with grand portraits. Michael stopped dead in his tracks, looking at the largest portrait. "That looks just like your father," Charles said. "That is my grandfather," Michael said softly.

Charles thought Michael did not know much about his father's side of the family. Charles also thought he knew more than Michael, but never said anything because it was learned through his parents. The man in the portrait was wearing a military uniform with several medals. "Very intimidating," Michael thought to himself.

"Down here, boys," came a voice from the other end of the hall. It was Tess, Michael's mother's secretary. Tess was a tall woman in her thirties and from The Hague or Amsterdam. Michael couldn't remember. "That is

Tess. Queen Wilhelmina picked her to be my mother's secretary," Michael informed him as they walk the rest of the way. The two sat down at the table and waited for the rest to arrive.

Roberts's secretary, Emma, walked in and acknowledged the boys and Tess. "The Earl and Countess will be arriving shortly, she said." Michael turned to his friend and whispered, "Tess came to London to help with the move. I have not met Emma yet. But father said she is helpful." Emma was average size, with tightly curled black hair. Her round eyeglasses made her face look just as rounded.

The six ate their lunch, and Michael's parents quizzed the boys on their plans for the day. Robert suggested they walk the old servants' passages, except for the third floor because it is the staff's private areas. Robert handed his son a key to unlock any of the passage doors. The boys were excused from the table and did not hesitate to start their assignment.

"Let's get some supplies," Michael suggested, feeling a true sense of adventure. The two walked up to Michael's room, where they opened a large trunk under one of the windows. "Torches, canteens, notebooks, pencils, compass, rucksack," Michael called out as he laid each item side by side on the floor while taking inventory. Michael held up the canteen. "We do not know how long we will be gone, so we should get some water for this first."

The boys walked to the water closet down the hall to fill the canteen. "We should sketch out a map of the passages," Charles suggested. "Excellent idea," Michael said in agreement. "I will bring my pocket watch, so we are not late," Charles suggested as they walked back to Charles' room. "Do you think this room has a passage door?" Charles asked as they walked in. Michael began pushing on the inner walls. "Ah!" he exclaimed as the hidden door opens. "It is in a different spot than my room."

"It is half-past one," Charles noted. "That gives us four hours, before we must meet your parents at six o'clock." Then he sighed heavily. "After we eat, I have to meet with my new teacher," completing his statement with an eye roll. Michael was less than excited to meet his new teacher. "I hope he is better than the one we had in London!"

Closing the door behind them, they immediately noticed this passage was different than the one connected to Michael's room. To their left, a flight of stairs descended downward. On their right, the stairs ascended to the second floor. "Up," Charles decided. "But remember that Father said not to go up to the third floor because it is the staff's living quarters." Michael always followed his father's directives.

After getting to the top of the stairs, they were greeted by a door that was ajar. They pushed it the rest of the way open to find a dimly lit red room. "Wow," the boys exclaimed in unison. "I think someone really liked red," finished Michael. The room was lined with bright red walls and a ceiling but was absent of furniture or art. The wood window shutters were open, but the windows were covered with a layer of dirt, not allowing much light through. "Does not look like anyone has been in here for years!" Charles said as he looked over every inch of the room.

The duo stepped into the hallway and looked side to side. This second level was different than the other two. The floors were bare wood and creaked as they walked up and down the hall, entering each room as they passed it. The last room was different than all the others, full of furniture and beautiful art. Eyeing an oversized desk a few feet away, Charles suggested they use it to lay out their paper and draw their map.

"Let's mark all of the passageways and where they go," Michael said. "Yes!" Charles agreed. They quickly decided to start with the floor they were on because they had already checked each room for the hidden doors leading to the servants' passageways. "Where is the secret door for this room?" Michael asked Charles. They both started to push on the walls, but they were not able to find it.

The boys looked around the dark wooden-walled room and noticed a drawing of a palace with "Soestdijk Palace" written on the bottom corner. "Ah, we should call it Soestdijk Kammer," Michael suggested, speaking in his limited Dutch. "What is kammer?" Charles asked him. "It means room in Dutch." Charles quickly agreed with the name and wrote it down in the space they drew on the map. "Well, now that we have completed the map for this floor, we should go down to the first floor," Michael said, Charles nodding his head in agreement.

They walked out and opened the door just down from their base of operations. "It looks like the servant's stairs," Charles stated. "Better not use these." Taking out the notepad, he sketched the servants' stairs onto it.

They went back to the red room's passageway and went all the way down. They passed the first floor and ended up in the basement. "Ah, the kitchen," Michael stated as he walked through the door.

There were two women sitting at the large table. "Hallo, Meneer Michael," said one woman. The boys walked into the kitchen and see the two women were identical twins. "Gosh!" gasped Charles, "I have never met twins before," he continued. The two women smiled. "How may we help you boys?" asked the second woman. "Father said to explore the house and passages," Michael replied. "How exciting," the sisters said at the same time.

Fleur was wearing a black uniform dress, and Cornelia was dressed in an all-white dress with an apron. "Must be the cook," Michael thought to himself. Fleur introduced herself, "I am Fleur, your family's head housekeeper," as she gave a quick bow to the boys.

She turned to introduce her sister. "This is my sister Cornelia, your family's head cook." Cornelia gave a quick bow and said, "You must be Lord Charles, I have received your food likes and dislikes from the Dutchess." The boys announced their pleasure to meet the twins, and Charles spoke up, "Lunch was the best!"

Cornelia turned and walked over to a tall cupboard. "You boys will need a snack while you explore." She pulled out pieces of various cakes, breads, and some fruits. She placed them into two small sacks and handed them to the boys.

Fleur gave them some tips on how to navigate the passages. "We still use them, but not nearly as much as they were used in the past." When Charles pulled out the map, they started drawing. Fleur explained that the first floor had the same passages as the second floor, but that they were in different areas of each room.

"Why does this room not have a passage?" asked Michael as he pointed to their base. Fleur smiles, "You didn't find it? There is one, but now I expect you to search again," Fleur chuckles. "There is one in there?" questioned the boys. "Oh, yes!" exclaimed Fleur. The boys looked at each other, confused because they had pushed on all the walls. "I will give you a hint, "Fleur continued. "It is not by the fireplace or even on the same side of the room.

"Fleur pointed over to a door next to the servants' dining room. "That door will take you up to the dining rooms upstairs." The boys thanked the twins once again and walked up the stairs that Fleur pointed out.

At the top of the stairs, they found two doors. One marked with "Groot" and one marked "Klein". Michael spoke up and said, "I know klein means small. Let us eat our snacks before going up to the first floor." As the boys sat down at the table to eat, Charles pulled out the notebook and told Michael, "I will add the information Fleur told us."

They heard voices in the hallway. Michael saw a large, fancy black motorcar sitting on the drive. "I wonder who is here?" pointing out the window. The boys walked over to the window and saw Robert with a well-dressed man. The stranger handed Robert an envelope and made a short bow to Robert before getting back into the motorcar.

As Robert walked back into the house, Michael and Charles ran into the hall. "Who was that, father?" Michael was excited. "The Queen's secretary," Robert replied with a smile. "Queen Wilhelmina's secretary?!" asked Michael with a confused look on his face. "Yes, she is planning a visit here in three weeks' time," Robert replied, with a smile on his face.

"Mary!" Robert called out. Tess stepped into the hall from the small study and into Robert's view. "Lady Mary is in the back garden, my lord," pointing in that direction. "Please get her for me, Oh-and ask for Emma and Lars as well." Robert handed the envelope to Tess, then turned and handed Michael the letter from that envelope. "It is in Dutch, father. But I know the Royal Warrant at the top," Michael continued. Robert nodded and took the letter back from his son.

"Oh, my!" exclaimed Charles, "You are about to have a Royal visit," he continued, still holding a slice of cake in his hands. Michael turned around and replied with only a shocking look on his face. "Why does the Queen want to visit?" Michael asked out loud to anyone who might give him the answer. From the other end of the hallway, Robert answered his son's question. "She is celebrating the transition in the House of Nassau."

Michael and Charles walked back into the small dining room. As they sat at the table, Charles asked, "Why do you, your father, and your late uncle have English names?" Michael swallowed the too-large of a bite of cake and replied, "My father's mother was English. Grandfather allowed his sons to have non-Dutch names because they were not religious." Charles shrugged his shoulders and mused, "I just thought it odd that your family is Dutch, but only your surname is Dutch."

The two sat at the dining table in the center of the small dining room. The room was lined with gold silk wall coverings, and the shutters were gilded in gold. A large crystal chandelier was centered over the table. Michael was sitting with his back to the large fireplace at the side of the room. Charles sat opposite his friend, drawing on their maps.

Michael and Charles reviewed their drawings. On the ground floor, they just had to complete adding the large dining room, which was in the original wing, whereas the small dining room they were in was connected to the formal dining room. The duo continued exploring once they finished eating their snacks.

"Look here," shouted Michael. "Our furniture from the London sitting room is in here." Robert and Mary like the Art nouveau style of furniture. The small sitting room was at the end of the original wing. "This room does not fit with any of the other rooms in the palace," giggled Michael. Blues and golds were the primary colors of the room. The Art Nouveau furniture was large and ornate but very modern compared to the centuries-old palace.

The entire ground floor had now been drawn into Michael's and Charles' notebook. "We should finish the first floor," suggested Charles. Michael placed the notebook back into his rucksack and the two walked down the large, vibrant hallway toward the grand staircase.

Chapter

3

Michael's family has a strong Dutch history. He is a cousin to the reigning monarch of the Kingdom of the Netherlands. He is the direct descendent of Prince William the Silent, who was assassinated by a sympathizer to the Spanish King. Prince William the Silent is the first of the House of Nassau.

Robert walked into the large study and sat at his desk. "My Lord, you have requested me?" announced Lars. "Yes, but I wish for the others to arrive before I make my announcement." Mary, Tess, and Emma walked through the large double doors into the large study. Robert stood up and cleared his throat. "My cousin, Queen Wilhelmina, has sent word that she will arrive in three weeks' time for a week-long visit."

Lars looked as if he was being chased by a wild horse. "My lord, what day did Her Majesty give as her arrival date?"

"She will arrive on the first of July," replied Robert. Mary stood up with a smile. "How exciting. I have not seen her in ages," said Mary. She continued, "Tess, Emma, and I will go below stairs and meet with the housekeeper immediately.

Mary led Emma and Tess to the kitchen to meet with Fleur. Robert and Lars planned for the visit. "My lord, may I ask how long ago it was that you last saw Her Majesty?" asked Lars, hoping not to overstep his bounds. "I saw her just before we arrived at the estate. We met several times before that to arrange the estate's staff to stay on, and to find new help for Michael and Lady Mary."

Michael and Charles walked up the main stairs to the first floor. Michael was still in shock about the recent news. "What time is it, Charles?" asked Michael. "It is five o'clock," he responded just as his pocket watched slipped from his hand. Bending over to pick it up and put it in his pocket, he noted a very tall man walking toward them.

It was the second footman, Antoon. "Hallo, Maneer Michael. Hallo, Lord Charles," he spoke and gave a quick bow. "Gentleman, Willem asked me to fetch you now because of the news of the Queen's visit." Michael was surprised the news made it that quickly to the house staff. Antoon guided the boys to the furthest back section of the estate on the first floor.

They ended at a large double door. Antoon turned the latch and opened it, through which Michael and Charles walked in to see Willem standing at attention wearing a dark grey suit. He gave a short bow and greeted Meneer Michael first.

"Sir, because of your cousin Queen Wilhelmina's announcement, I wanted to meet you before the evening meal." He turned and greeted Charles. "Sir, the Duke and Duchess sent word that you will attend some of the education with Meneer Michael during your stay."

The look Charles gave him must have been a look of dread, because Willem held up a hand and smiled. "Meneer Michael and Meneer Charles, this education during the summer will be purely informal. I strongly feel that the summer months will be for a young person's relaxation and enjoyment."

The two boys relaxed slightly. "What type of education is it, then?" asked Michael. Willem stepped over to a row of portraits, maps, and books. "These will help me teach you boys the history of Michael's family, the House of Nassau, and more Dutch." He turned to Michael. "I understand you know some Dutch already." Michael walked closer to look at the things laid out. "I know basic Dutch only," he said as he moved the items around.

Willem walked over to a desk and picked up a piece of paper. "This is a small agenda I have planned for you both. Nothing crazy for the summer, but important for the two of you to understand." He looked at Michael. "The Earl and Countess include you in more things than any other aristocrats I have worked with before."

He smiled and handed the paper to Michael. "I find it very nice that your parents do not exclude you from these types of things," Charles spoke up quickly. "I am glad my parents do not allow me to take part in their boring lives." Willem turned to him and asked, "Are you ready to be the next Duke, sir?" Charles became pale and emphatically exclaimed, "No!"

"Well, Meneer Charles, I am sad to say that Meneer Michael will be more prepared to inherit his title and estate than you will be with yours." Willem commented with, "Now go enjoy the rest of your day and follow that agenda I gave you. I will see you in two days in this room." Michael and Charles walked out and headed toward their rooms.

Michael turned to Charles and said, "Sorry your parents are lumping you into all of this." Charles looked at Michael with a smile. "Based on this, I am looking forward to it. I will learn more about your family and some Dutch."

At six o'clock, the boys walked down the main stairs and into the small dining room. Inside, they saw a fully dressed table with everyone already sitting down. "Hello, mother, father, Prime Minister," said Michael as he took his seat. Charles sat next to his friend and leaned over to whisper, "That is the Dutch Prime Minister?"

"Yes," Michael said without turning his head. "His name is Charles Ruijs de Beerenbrouck."

Michael had met the Dutch Prime Minister several

times before. Robert was sitting to the Prime Minister's right, and Mary was on his left. Michael and Charles were sitting across from them. The four footmen brought the food to the table, starting with Robert. Lars began pouring the wine at the same time. Mary let out a slight giggle and said, "No work talk while we eat." Prime Minister de Beerenbrouck replied quickly, with a slight grin on his face. "I do not enjoy discussing work while eating, it causes an upset stomach."

"Meneer Michael and Lord Charles," the Prime Minister said, addressing the duo, "How is your summer thus far?" Michael replied first, "Not terrible, but not great either." Charles had a different response. "I am excited to be here instead of Belgium with my parents, sir."

Robert looked at his son with some concern. "Why not, great my son?" Michael, realizing his response was less than ideal, replied, "Well, father, I am in a new home, which is fun, but last summer we went to the sea every day." Mary smiled and let out the same sweet giggle and said, "We will go later in the summer when things settle more."

The Prime Minister was sensitive to Michael's response. "I totally understand, Meneer Michael. And now your cousin, Her Majesty, has announced a visit." Michael sat up a little straighter and smiled. "I am excited to see her again, sir." Michael continued while arranging the food on his dish, "She has always been kind to me and never treats me like a child." The Prime Minister nodded in agreement. "She is indeed a wonderful monarch and woman."

They spent the hour eating a wonderful meal. Tess walked in, but Lars stopped her quickly, "The family is eating and is not to be disturbed," he stated in an authoritative voice. "I have a telegram for her ladyship," replied Tess. Lars held out his hand, waiting for Tess to hand it over. Tess looked at him with disapproval but handed it to him, nonetheless. Lars motioned to Tess to leave and whispered, "Never overstep you bounds with me, especially when it comes to protocol." The private secretaries would have normally eaten with the family unless they had guests. Lars placed the telegram onto a small tray, walked over to Mary, and stood slightly behind her on the left with the tray extended.

He whispered, "My Lady, a telegram." Mary took it with no one noticing. After reading it, she placed it on the table next to her dish.

Once Robert and the Prime Minister completed their conversation, she spoke up. "The Duke and Duchess have sent a telegram." While looking at Charles, she continued, "Your parents will arrive by train in ten days. They are requesting that they stay here for a week before they continue to London." Charles smiled and replied with "That will be nice. I wonder why they are shortening their holiday?"

The group walked into the grand library for drinks for the adults, and books for Michael and Charles. Mary handed the telegram to Lars and instructed him to reply to the telegram that the rooms would be ready. "Lars," Mary said, "Can you also please ask the house staff to make sure the Prince William of Orange rooms are ready for the Duke and Duchess." Lars bowed and walked to the servant's stairs leading to the kitchen.

Mary turned to Robert and informed him that the staff will prepare the Queen's rooms tomorrow. Hearing this, Michael chimed up, "What rooms will Her Majesty be staying in?" Mary smiled and said, "The first floor has apartments dedicated to the monarch at the top of the stairs on the left." Michael was thinking a moment and said, "Charles and I have not been in those rooms yet."

The Prime Minister asked Michael, "Have you been exploring much?" Michael and Charles put down their books and walked over to the three adults. "Oh, Yes! Father told us to start with the servants' passages. We have set up in a room on the second floor to draw a map of the house." Robert, with excitement, asked, "What room have you set base in?" Michael sat on the arm of his father's chair. "We are calling it the Soestdijk Kammer, father. It is the room next to the servants' stairs."

Robert thought for a moment. "Ah! That was my old teacher's room. I did not like her much; she was mean – and French." It was well known that French teachers were quite strict and demanding of their students, and Robert's experience had been no different. Robert continued, "Speaking of teachers, have you met your new one yet?" Michael sighed slightly, "Yes, father, he seems nice enough. And he is not French – he is Dutch."

"Her Majesty would not have it any other way!" the Prime Minister declared, then cleared his throat.

Michael stood up and walked over to the Prime Minister. "Did Her Majesty arrange for my new teacher?" The Prime Minister blushed slightly, "She did. She wanted to make sure her cousins were well taken care of." Concluding their conversation, Michael and Charles walked back to the beautifully upholstered colonial-style chairs where they placed their books. The boys had found their favorite authors, respectively.

The Prime Minister adjusted himself in his armchair to see Robert better. "Robert, I want to thank you for accepting this new position for me. Her Majesty is extremely grateful, as with your father's death, she needs to have an ally in her government." Robert appeared uncomfortable and paused thoughtfully before he spoke. "I understand the importance of the Nassau name and this house. I may have some animosity toward my late father, but…" The Prime Minister held up his hand and nodded in understanding.

Concerned, Mary looked at the Prime Minister and inquired, "Does her Majesty need an ally in government?" Overhearing the conversation, Michael and Charles' interest was piqued and they rejoined the others. The Prime Minister shrugged, "All monarchs need an ally in their government. I even need an ally or two being Prime Minister."

Looking to Robert, Charles asked, "Sir, does that put a great deal of stress on you?" Then added, "I am glad my father is not in your position!" Robert let out a loud, short laugh. "My dear Charles, your father is in my position. Your father is a Duke….a PEER. What do you think a Peer is?" He continued, "A Peer in British

Parliament is the King's ally in his government." Charles paused thoughtfully. "King Albert needs an ally….I guess I have never thought about father's work before." Robert and the Prime Minister smiled. Charles' opinion of his father changed instantly. This is the first time he had any interest in what his father did. "I shall talk with my father when he arrives, so I can learn more!"

Robert and the Prime Minister smiled. Charles' opinion of his father changed to being proud and strong. This is the first time he had any interest in what his father did. "I shall talk with my father when he arrives, so I can learn more!" Michael looked at his friend and began to laugh. "I guess we have a lot to learn about each other's family now!"

Robert, Mary, and the Prime Minister began a conversation that did not interest the boys. They walked over and grabbed their books. "We should go up and work on our maps," suggested Michael to Charles. They opened the hidden passage behind a large bookcase. The two remembered the path well and ended up in Soestdijk Kammer.

"Charles, we should organize this room, then look for that door." Charles nodded in agreement, and they arranged the room to suit their needs. They placed the large desk in the center of the room and pulled up two chairs to the desk.

A few moments later, Fleur arrived from behind a large portrait of one of the former kings. "Hallo, jongens," Fleur shouted slightly to scare them. Both jumped and looked over to find her. "I am guessing you never found the passage in this room," Fleur said with a smile. She turned around, not allowing them to respond, and closed the door behind her. Michael looked surprised and defeated as well. "Well, damn!" Michael shouted.

Chapter

4

Michael and Charles awoke early the following day. He looked at the clock on his mantel and noted the time. The morning meal would not be ready for another hour. Michael opened the massive shutters to all four windows. As his eyes scanned the landscape below, he had an odd feeling that something did not feel right. He shrugged it off and walked through the passage connecting his room to Charles' as the clock chimed the hour. Charles was still in bed, but awake.

"How did you sleep?" asked Michael. Charles stretched and swung his legs to the side, "Like the dead, I think. This bed is not from the 1600's luckily," he chuckled. Michael began opening the window shutters in his friend's room. "It is too early for breakfast, as it is only seven o'clock." Charles walked over to the chair and put on his dressing gown. "Can we go down in our pajamas? Charles asked. Michael shrugged, "We did in London, so I do not see why we cannot here."

The duo went through to Michael's room and walked down to his father's study using the hidden passage. As they stepped through the door, they saw Robert and Lars talking by the massive doors. Robert turned, "Boys, please come here," as he motioned them over.

"Lars has informed me that a footman is missing, but all of his belongings are still in his rooms." The boys gave a look of intrigue, and Michael asked which footman was missing. "It is Antoon," said Lars. "Oh! He took me to Willem and brought me the note from mother saying Charles was coming to stay," Michael told his father. "Lars, take me and the boys up to Antoon's rooms, please," as Robert was directing the boys to follow. Lars took them to the servants' stairs at the end of the great hall. The servant's rooms were on the third floor.

At the top of the stairs, they were met with two separate doors. To the left was for the female staff, and to the right was for the male staff. Lars had the keys for the male side, and Fleur had the ones for the female side. This prevented the sexes from mixing. Lars opened the first door on the left.

The door tag had "Antoon—Second Footman" written on it. Michael walked in first, followed by Charles, then Robert. Lars explained the staff had two connecting rooms each. The first was their sitting room with a bedroom connected.

"I let myself in after no answer to my knocking, your

Lordship," Lars explained. "I expected him to be ill or still sleeping, but he is not here," he continued. Michael and Charles looked around as Lars and Robert continued discussing Antoon. "Very plain," thought Michael. The walls were all white with basic furniture. Michael could see four armchairs with several small tables in the sitting room, and some photos of what he assumed were Antoon's family.

Charles and Michael walked into the bedroom. "His regular clothing is still here, father," Michael announced. A single-person bed and a dresser filled the small room. On the small bedside table, there sat Antoon's wallet. On the bed lay several items of clothing neatly placed. Robert asked Lars, "Is he responsible? Should we be concerned?" Lars indeed had an expression of concern when he stated, "I count on and trust him more than any other house staff, my lord."

Robert directed the male staff to search the estate, including the cottages. "Lars, contact the outside staff to search the outbuildings and grounds?" Lars bowed and turned to the phone on the wall in the servants' hall. He spoke to the telephone operator, "Please connect me to the estate manager of Palace Nassau. This is the butler."

Robert turned to the boys, "I want you to walk all the servants' passages, go from the attic to the kitchens. I give you permission to cross staff lines for this." The first footman went to Robert and bowed, "My Lord, my room is next to Antoon's, and I heard what sounded like him falling into bed late last night."

"What time?" asked Robert. "I was already asleep, and the sound woke me. I just went back to sleep without checking the time, my lord." Robert nodded in response. Lars ended the phone call, "I told Meneer Jan the situation. He said he and his staff will search immediately." Robert thanked him. "I have instructed my son and the Marquess to assist in the search. I normally tell them to avoid the staff area, but I have given them permission to be in ALL areas." Lars bowed in understanding and began his own search. "Where should we start?" asked Charles. Michael looked at him and suggested, "We should split up and divide the passages."

Charles thought a moment, "Good idea, let's meet up in Soestdijk Kammer in half an hour. Do you have your pocket watch?" Michael went to his room, opened the box on one of his bedside tables, and pulled out a gold pocket watch. The two made sure of the time and set off on their separate ways.

Robert went down to the first floor to find Mary in their rooms. The main bedroom was one of the largest rooms on the first floor. Mary was sitting in her dressing gown, putting on her house shoes. Her lady's maid was going over her morning agenda with the Countess. "Mary," Robert walked through the main bedroom door. "Good morning, dear." The last part sounding more like a question when she noticed Robert's expression.

"Whatever is wrong, Robert? Are the boys.....alright?" Mary asking with concern now in her voice. "They are fine," replied Robert. "Lotte," Exclaimed Robert to

Mary's lady's maid, "Please find Fleur and get further instructions. One of the footmen is missing, and we are searching the estate." Robert turned to Mary. "I have the boys helping in the search. I will get dressed and help with the search outside."

"What shall I do, dear?" As Robert fastened his shirt, he replied, "One of the family should remain in the public areas. If anyone finds him or has questions, there should be one of us available." Mary understood and dressed quickly. Mary walked down to the small study and pulled the bell cord.

A few minutes later, Emma and Tess walked into the study. Mary looked up and asked, "Have you ladies heard the news of the footman?" Emma and Tess both responded in the affirmative simultaneously. "The Earl is out on the estate helping the outdoors staff look for the footman. His Lordship has also recruited Meneer Michael and the Marquess in the searching inside the house."

Fleur walked into the study. "You called my lady?" Mary turned around. "I have, and was hoping to get something small for the morning meal if possible. Can you see that there is some for the Earl and the boys?" Fleur bowed and said, "I have started the arrangements since getting the news from Lars, my lady. My sister is cooking it now and will bring it up shortly." Mary smiled, "Thank you, and thank your sister for me!" Michael and Charles met up in their base of operations.

Michael arrived first and sat at the desk. Michael acknowledged the 'off' feeling he had when he woke up this morning. When Charles walked in, Michael suggested they take the passage down to the kitchen. Charles pulled the portrait's frame from the hidden door, and the duo walked down. This passage connects to the basement, ground floor, first floor, second floor, and the third floor. Once down in the kitchen, they saw Cornelia loading a tray and being helped by Fleur.

Fleur noticed them. "Can you boys help carry the food trays up to the small study please?" Michael grabbed one and Charles grabbed the second. Fleur carried a tray with the drinks, while Cornelia opened the doors for them all.

The boys set the trays of food on a table in Mary's study. Mary hugged Michael and greeted him, asking how he slept. Michael smiled and kissed her cheek. "I slept very well, thank you. Much quieter here than in London." She turned to Charles with a smile, "And how did you sleep?" He responded to her the same way he had responded to Michael earlier. Mary laughed, "Imagine a mattress from 1620."

Mary sat at the table and ate some food and drank some tea. "Boys, go get dressed after eating some breakfast. Once your father returns, he will tell you what to do next." They agreed and helped themselves.

Cornelia had made Dutch pancakes and some pastries. Tess and Emma were sitting down with them to eat when Lars came to the door. "My lady, there is a telephone call from the Prime Minister for his lordship, but he still has not returned from his search. Shall I ask him to telephone back?" Mary thought a moment,

"Yes, please inform the Prime Minister of the situation, and that the Earl will telephone him back when he returns." Lars bowed and left the room.

"Mother, what do you think happened to Antoon?" Michael asked, not suspecting anything being amiss. "I have not a clue."

"I wonder if he just packed up and left." Michael was quick to tell his mother that all of his things are still in his rooms.

Emma chimed in and said, "I was talking with him last evening, my lady. He told me that he was very happy to remain with your family. I cannot think of a reason for him to leave after telling me this." Mary shook her head to agree that it does not make sense he would leave. "Do you know Antoon well?" Mary asked Emma. "No, my lady, he has been with your family for five years, but I have only been assigned as secretary to the Earl for six months now. I arrived to House Nassau the same day you and the family did." Mary looked over to Tess as if asking the same question. "I met him the same day as you, your ladyship."

Robert walked through and sat at the small table with everyone. He looked at Michael. "Did you find anything in the passages?" Michael and Charles shook their heads in response. "Any signs of him around?" Robert continued. "No, father, it is like he vanished." Robert sighed and drank some of the coffee. Mary placed her hand on Robert's. "Lars mentioned the Prime Minister phoned for you earlier. I told Lars to let the Prime Minister know the situation, and that you would phone him back when you could." Robert stood up and kissed his wife, then picked up the telephone, and waited for the operator to answer.

"This is the Earl Nassau. Please get me the Prime Minister's office." The boys stood up and went up to their rooms to change. They met in the main hallway and came up with their plan. Michael told his friend about the 'off' feeling he had when he woke up this morning. Just then, they saw one of the housemaids walking down the hall and into one of the passages. The boys followed. Noticing them, the housemaid sought to get out of their way and turned to leave.

"Stop!" cried the boys. "We want to talk to you about Antoon." The maid turned around, "I hope he is alright," she said. "So do we," Michael replied. "Do you know where he would go?" She thought a moment and said, "There is a place in Delft that he visits on his off days. He also goes to Gouda to see his mother." The boys thanked her, turned, and ran all the way to Mary's study. "Father! Father!" Michael yelled, almost out of breath. "What is it, my dear boy?" Robert asked while catching Michael. There is a maid who said Antoon goes to Gouda to visit his mother or Delft on his off days."

"Good show, my boy, those detective books will make you a regular sleuth," Robert said with a smile. Robert turned to his secretary, "Emma, please go give that information to Lars, and see if we need to go to Antoon's mothers." Emma stood and went down to the butler's office below stairs.

Michael caught his breath. "Father, what shall Charles and I do now?" Robert and Mary looked at each other, then at the boys. Mary said, "Go ask Fleur what you can do to help get ready for Her Majesty's visit. Tell her I sent you and do as Fleur tells you. "Right away, mother," Michael replied. The two went down to find Fleur.

The boys went below stairs but could not find Fleur. They saw Emma walking out of Lars' office and coming toward them. "I told Lars your information, and he is sending inquiries to Antoon's mother's house in Gouda. He does not think she has a telephone."

"Emma, what do you think happened to Antoon?" She merely shrugged her shoulders as she headed back up to Mary's study. Just as Emma left, Fleur walked up to them. "Hallo heren, how may I help you?"

"We are here to help you," Charles replied. Fleur looked puzzled. "Help me?" Michael spoke up, "Mother told us to ask you what you need help with to prepare for Queen Wilhelmina's visit." Fleur thought a few moments. "Come with me to the Royal Suite, and we will see." She turned and signaled for them to follow her up.

The three walked into the second-largest rooms of the estate on the first floor. The estate faced east, and the suite was on the southeast corner. None of the window shutters had been opened, and the heavy curtains were still closed. Fleur turned on the lights, which revealed the most regal room the boys had ever seen. "Wow!" They exclaimed.

Above a large fireplace was a portrait of Queen Wilhelmina. Fleur pointed to it, "We changed it to the Queen when she was crowned. Your late grandfather was happy to see it painted." The boys continued to look around. There was a portrait of Prince William of Orange next to the doors to the rooms. "My family is proud of him," Michael stated as he pointed to the portrait. Fleur turned and replied, "Your grandfather was most proud to be a direct descendent of his. You will find his portraits all over the estate."

The first room was a grand sitting area. Sofas, chairs, tables, and bookcases. This area was set up similarly to Mary's study. The walls were covered with the most vibrant blue and white silk coverings. The drapes are the same shade of blue. Michael connected it to the Royal Delft Blue history of the royal family and told Charles the significance of Delft, the color, and Prince William of Orange-Nassau.

Fleur opened two large doors from the sitting room. They led to the bedroom and the connected water closet and bedroom. This was one of the few rooms with its own facilities. The bedroom walls were lined with previous Dutch Kings and Queens. There was also a portrait of the current Prime Minister and Michael's late grandfather. Fleur sighed, "There are several pieces of furniture in storage that will need to come down. Also, we need to get the dust covers off everything else. Will you boys go to the attics and get the furniture I will need?"

Michael and Charles nodded in succession. "Good, I will tell you where and what to bring down." Fleur informed the boys how to get up to the attics, and which pieces to bring down, directing them to be most carful in their tasks.

Michael and Charles did as they were instructed. In total, they delivered ten small to medium sized furniture pieces. When they were finished, they were greeted by the three house maids. Each one was dressing in all white, including their aprons. "Those must be difficult to keep clean," said Michael. Fleur laughed. "Not when you have a few secrets up your sleeve." She handed the boys several kilograms of linens used as dust covers. "Please take these down to the laundry.

It is the third door past my office. You can take the servant's stairs down, and it will be on your left-hand side. When you're done with that, I don't think there is anything else you can do from here. Thank you!"

Michael opened the door to the laundry. When they walked in, they saw what looked like spilled red paint on the floor. Charles walked over to the side where the empty baskets were located. "Be careful," shouted Michael. He pointed to a knife on the floor with the same red on the blade.

"Go!—Go get my father!" directed Michael to Charles. Charles ran as fast as he could up the servants' stairs and over to the small study. It was empty. He switched over to the large study, but it was also empty. Charles ran room to room, not finding anyone. He finally found the Earl and Countess with Lars in the Delft room.

The room was filled with new and antique Delft porcelain. "Sir!" yelled Charles, out of breath. Startled, Robert, Mary, and Lars turned around. "Michael and I found blood and a bloodied knife in the laundry!" Charles was panting and out of breath. Robert could tell by the look on Charles' face that he was not making this story up. Robert turned to Mary. "Please finish up here while I find out what has happened." Mary nodded, and Robert kissed her forehead. He then turned to Lars and directed him and Charles to take him down to the laundry.

Chapter

5

Michael continued to stare at the floor. "That is not paint," he muttered to himself. Suddenly, it was dark. Someone covered his head with a cloth and wrapped a binding around his arms. He tried to scream but a large and very strong hand covered his mouth. He started kicking and screaming, but still nothing more than muffled sounds came out. Whoever had a hold of him was tall, as his feet were no longer on the ground.

A male voice demanded, "Silence or you die!" It was a voice he had never heard before and had an unfamiliar accent. There was the click of a door latch. He was thrown over the man's shoulder and they were now outdoors. Suddenly, they were on the ground. Whoever had him fell while running. Michael knew he was badly injured, as the person landed hard on top of him. Michael felt dizzy, and his head and neck were hurting. Michael could hear yelling and screaming in

Dutch. There was a scuffling sound in the grass, then someone was untying him and asking him if he was alright. Suddenly, the hood came off, and the sun blinded him. The man asked, "Meneer Michael, gaat het wel goed?" Michael looked up to see one of the main groundskeepers holding him. He looked back to see several men chasing someone in all black across the fields.

"Meneer!" The man repeated, "Gaat het wel goed?" Michael replied with "Ik spreek een beetje Nederlands." This means I speak some Dutch. The groundskeeper switched to English. "Are you alright?" Michael let the man hold him up. He was confused, scared, and dizzy. The man yelled, "Over here, my lord." Michael saw his father running toward them, then felt his arms embrace him tightly. He did not feel well. "My boy, are you alright?" Michael was still at a loss for what just happened, and could only stare at his father and faintly mutter, "No." This would be the last Michael spoke for a while.

Lars went to their side. He asked the groundskeeper what had happened. It was pure luck that he saw a man dressed in all black and his face covered carrying Michael. "I saw legs and shoes, then I saw that there was a sack over the boy's head and his arms were tied. My men and I started to chase when the man fell. He kept running and my men are chasing him now." The groundskeeper pointed to the door at the back of the house, "They came out from there." Lars looked over to see the door to the laundry.

Robert carried Michael like a small child up to the

entrance and into the house. He screamed out, "BEL ONMIDDELLIJK DE RIJKSPOLITIE!" Robert was so upset he went into speaking Dutch to his secretary. Mary came to his side immediately and took Michael away from Robert. Charles was already in the large study terrified and ran to be with his best friend. "Michael! Are you alright?!" shouted Charles. Michael still had not responded to anyone. Laying in his mother's arms still in shock with what happened. He was trying to wrap his mind around what he saw.

Robert took the telephone away from Emma and was yelling into it. He was still speaking Dutch. "Emma," shouted Mary, "What is the Earl saying?" Mary's Dutch was as basic as Michael's. "His lordship demanded we telephone the police, and he is speaking to them now. At that point, Lars walked into the room.

Robert turned to him and yelled, "Lock this palace down! Nobody in or out until the police arrive!" Mary, very confused and now scared. "What is happening?" she cried. Robert turned to his wife. "Someone attempted to kidnap our boy."

"What?" Mary still had the look of confusion, and then sadness developed.

Lars pulled the bell cord and rapidly shut each window shutter to the study. Two footmen arrived. "His lordship has ordered to lock down the palace." They separated and closed every window shutter, latched every exterior door, and a footman was station outside the main entrance to wait for the police and act as a lookout should the kidnappers return.

The Palace Nassau was thirty minutes from The Hague in South Holland Province. Roberts made a few more telephone calls, then sat next to Mary and Michael. Charles was still trying to talk to his best friend. And Michael still was not talking to anyone: he was just staring up to the ceiling.

After what felt like hours, they heard several cars pulling up to the drive. The footman stationed outside pulled the bell to signal their arrival. Robert stood up and walked to the main entrance.

The Royal Police arrived, and Robert meets the commanding officer at the door. Charles could not hear what they were saying, but several uniformed officers scatted about the estate.

A few minutes later, a large black car arrived. A man in a dark blue suit stepped into the study and bowed. It was the Minister of Defense. "My lord, I have requested the Royal Marechaussee to be dispatched here as well. I hope you do not mind me taking that liberty." Robert shook his head and focused on Michael and Charles. "Charles, are you alright?"

"I…..I…..I am not sure, sir." Charles looked up and continued, "Michael is not talking. He looks at me but will not talk."

Bas, the Minister of Defense, walked over to Robert. "Sir, shall I telephone a doctor for the boy to make sure he is well?" Bas had a strong loyalty to the Nassau family. He worked for Robert's late father, also the Minister of Defense. Robert looked up, "Please Bas, thank you." Bas walked to the desk and telephoned for the Royal physician.

Over a dozen Marechaussee vehicles arrived. "What is Marechaussee?" Charles asked openly. Bas was the one who replied. "They are Royal military with police powers. They protect Her Majesty and the royal palaces." He continued, "I felt it necessary due to the Nassau family being cousins to Her Majesty." Robert stood up. "I think our missing footman may be connected to this." Bas turned to him, "What missing footman?" Robert explained that one of the footmen was missing and that the butler was worried because it was out of character for the man.

A knock on the study doors broke the conversation. Bas walked over and opened it. There was Willem, Michael's new teacher. Willem noticed it was Bas, and he took a half step back and saluted him. Bas was confused. Willem introduced himself as the new teacher for the young Michael but explained he was retired Royal Dutch Army and Marechaussee. Bas saluted him back.

"My lord, may Willem enter?" Robert nodded and motioned for him to enter. "I know you do not live in the house, Willem, but I am asking you as a personal favor to move in and protect the boys and my wife." He did not let him answer and turned to Bas. "I want Willem armed and give him whatever he requires. I want him to have it without question!" Robert was well versed in Willem's training in the military. Willem even served with the Royal Marechaussee briefly before retirement. This is partially why the Queen sent him to the Nassau household as Michael's teacher. "Is he alright my lord?" asked Willem, looking at Michael. "A physician has been called to check him; he has not spoken since the rescue." Robert, looking at Michael, continued, "I do not care what it takes. Find the man who tried to abduct my son."

Bas guided Willem out of the room and into the entry hall. The commanding officer of the Royal Police was there and walked over to the two men. Bas spoke first and introduced Willem. "I want you to arm him and give him any supplies and resources he requires. The Royal Police Inspector saluted the men and said he would return shortly. As he walked out the door, the Prime Minister walked in.

Walking towards the study, the Prime Minister noticed the two and pointed them to follow him into the study. The Prime Minister was the last to enter and closed the door behind him.

"I may be the Prime Minister," he said, looking at Robert. "But you and your family are the blood and soul of the country. You may be my personal secretary, but you are also the Earl Nassau and the cousin to Her Majesty the Queen. This is officially a political attempted kidnapping until proven otherwise. Robert, you are officially my boss from this point, and I will do whatever you need me or our government to do." Robert only said, "Find them!"

Robert took Michael from Mary and carried him up to his room and placed him into his bed. Charles and Mary had followed behind them. Willem walked in and knocked on the door. Robert turned and acknowledged him. "My lord, it is my understanding that there are several passages in the house." Charles handed Willem the notebook sitting on Michael's bedside table. "Here, sir, this has maps we drew of all of the passages. "Good show," Robert said. Looking up to Willem, he introduced Charles, stating, "This is the Marquess of Luxly. His father is the Duke of Luxly. You are to guard him as well as my son. The Duke and Dutchess are already on their way, but will not arrive for several more days." Willem bowed and promised to protect the entire family as well as the Marquess.

Mary walked over to the bell cord and pulled several times. A few moments later, Lars arrived. Mary looked at him and said as any normal mother would, "Please get my son some soup and tea. He is not well after this." Lars bowed, saying, "I will get the entire family something, my lady," and left the room. Mary was at a loss for what to do or say, even.

"Marquess, would you be willing to move from your room to Meneer Michaels?" Willem asked. "Of course, I want to be close to my friend, anyhow." Willem then addressed Robert. "My lord, may I move my things into the room the young Marquess was in? Robert halfway looked at Willem and replied, "Good idea."

Chapter
6

Robert stood up from Michael's bed and announced that he would be down in his study. Mary quickly took his place on Michael's bed and said nothing. Charles went through the passage to the room he was staying in to move his things over. As Charles was moving his items, he could hear a small commotion in the hall.

When he peaked his head out the door, he saw several uniformed Royal Police and the Marechaussee walking down the hall. Willem stepped out and closed the door to Michael's room and locked it.

The Dutch Prime Minister, Major for the Royal Marechaussee, and the Inspector with the Royal Police were meeting in the large study. Robert pushed the large double doors open, causing all three to turn towards him rapidly. All three bowed, but Robert held his hand up, preventing them from speaking.

"The Marquess and my son were in the laundry when they discovered a puddle of blood and a bloody knife. Michael sent the Marquess alert me and alert me to their findings. I immediately followed the Marquess to the laundry to find the blood and the knife, but Michael was not there. Lars was with us, and we heard a commotion outdoors."

"Where is the laundry, my lord?" asked Inspector Jan Jansen. "I will take all of you there", Robert turned and opened the hidden passage door next to the fireplace. The men walked down to the basement and down the hall to the laundry. The Major of the Royal Marechaussee walked into the laundry first.

"That is a significant amount of blood," said Major Daan Dekker. Inspector Jansen, the Prime Minister, and Robert followed him in. "Where is the knife?" asked Inspector Jansen. Robert directed them to the right of the laundry bags. A long kitchen knife with blood on the blade and handle was lying on the floor. The two piles of linen dropped by Michael and Charles were still on the floor.

"We must seal off the basement and this room!" demanded Inspector Jansen. Robert directed the men around the corner to the door that leads to the back gardens of the estate. "This is where the groundskeeper said they saw the man running with my son." Robert continued, "I heard the commotion outdoors and found the staff holding Michael."

The men inspected the door and find tool marks on the lock and door. "I realize this is how he made entry," claimed Major Daan Dekker. The Inspector quickly chimed up, "I agree, Major, but a person would have to know the area and where this door leads." Dekker turned to Robert, "My Lord, who would know where this door leads or is even here?"

"You would have to ask the staff" Robert continued as he walked to Lars, "I have not been in this house for almost twenty years gentleman."

"Lars, I want you to be available for the Royal Police and the Marechaussee." The butler bowed to the Earl and replied while standing ever more at attention, "Anything for you and the family, my lord!" Lars turned to the Inspector and Major with, "Only staff would know that door existed." Someone in the background spoke up. "My lord, I suggest we move you and the family to Dam Palace in Amsterdam." Robert turned quickly, and his body language and tone changed, "ABSOLUTELY NOT!"

"I am the Earl Nassau. My entire family lived here, and it is where we will stay. YOU gentlemen are tasked with finding the devil and to protect my family at the same time." Robert could not tell which of the men recommended the move to Dam Palace. Everyone bowed even more, noting the difference they saw in Robert.

The Prime Minister placed a hand on his friend's shoulder. "The Major and the Inspector will move their men into the estate immediately."

"I will take the Earl to the large study, as you plan," as

he looked at the two men. Major Dekker and Inspector Jansen nodded in agreement.

As the Prime Minister walked his friend upstairs, the two looked at Lars. Major Dekker spoke, "Lars, we need to move several Royal Police and Marechaussee into the palace. We also need to establish a command room. Can you please help us make these arrangements?

Lars nodded and directed the two up to the second floor. As they go to the first set of empty rooms, he points to the servant's staircase. "In the attics, you will find several beds, tables, and chairs. I will have the footmen bring them down today." Lars continued, there are three water closets and two bathrooms on this level. I will have the housekeeper arrange for them to be ready as well." Major Dekker and Inspector Jansen nodded in agreement.

"This will work well for us Lars," said Jansen. "Are there a couple rooms in the basement that we may use as an office and interview room?" asked Dekker. The butler thought and suggested the old cook's rooms in the basement. "The current cook lives with her sister in one of the estate cottages." Lars continued, "The old cook's rooms are three rooms with only one door into them, located in the back of the basement." Lars took the two down to show them the rooms. The old cook's rooms included a bedroom, a sitting area, and an office. All three had one door in and out. Each of the rooms had a small window allowing outside light into the rooms. "This will work well for our command room," said Dekker. Inspector Jansen agreed. "Are there any spare beds?" Lars thought a moment, "I also live in one of the estate cottages. The old butler lived in the rooms connected to my office. We can move that bed into here for you." Inspector Jansen and Major Dekker knew that this would require them to stay on the estate for an unknown amount of time. Jansen sat in one of the chairs, "I think we should call for Johannes de Groot," he said with a sigh. Dekker nodded and sat next to Jansen. "This definitely requires de Groot's skills." Lars knocked on the door and let himself in.

"I have instructed the house staff to prepare ten rooms on the second floor. I have also instructed them to move another bed here. They will have everything ready for you and your men in two hours." Dekker stood, shook Lars' hand, and thanked him.

"We will need to interview all the staff, and no one shall pass the staff dining room. The laundry is strictly out of bounds, and the door in question shall be out of bounds" he said decidedly. A uniformed Royal Policeman was stationed by the laundry and back door. Inspector Jansen called the Royal Police headquarters and ordered Brigadier Johannes de Groot to be dispatched to Palace Nassau immediately.

As Jansen placed the telephone receiver down, he could hear two women talking in the kitchen and Dekker. Cornelia was in the kitchen with one of her kitchen maids. "Hallo Mevrouw Cornelia," Dekker said with a smile. Cornelia turned around to see an old friend she knew only as Daan. "Daan!" she exclaimed while hugging her old friend. "I expect you are high ranking now with the Marechaussee," she continued. "I am now Major, my dear." Dekker still smiling at Cornelia.

"The entire staff are scared Daan!" As Major Dekker calmed his old friend, Inspector Jan Jansen, walked into the kitchen.

"Having a reunion, I hear," said Jansen. "We grew up together in Gouda" explained Dekker. "We will still need to interview her Major," snapped Jansen. "I will make sure the Royal Police interview her as well as her sister and not the Marechaussee" Dekker was quick to snap back.

Cornelia explained that the evening meal was almost ready for the family. "We eat after the family is served. I make double, so we eat the same as the family. We will have enough for only a few extra to eat with us below stairs." The Major and the Inspector looked at each other just now, realizing there will be several extra mouths to feed. "Major, we will have many men here for an unknown amount of time. Should we contact extra kitchen help?"

Jansen looked at Cornelia and then Major for some kind of answer.

"Cornelia, I will call headquarters to have them send one of the military cooks tonight. They will cook for the Marechaussee and Royal Police staff, so you will not have to cook extra." Dekker turned to look around. "Is there a space for the extra supplies and staff?"

Cornelia smiled and directed Dekker and Jansen to a closed door. "Open that and tell me," she replied. Jansen pulled open the door to see a second kitchen. "Another kitchen?" Asked the men. "This is a palace, after all, and if there is a royal visit, the monarch brings their own cooks. So yes, I think we can handle the extra kitchen staff and supplies."

Major Dekker contacted the Marechaussee headquarters in The Hague. He was able to be assigned two cooks, some kitchen staff, and food supplies. After the telephone call ended, he turned to Jansen. "Her Majesty has sent word that we have any resource we needed at any time." Jansen nodded, "I am sure we do."

Lars walked over to the Major. "Sir, Fleur has told me that the second floor will be stocked with linen within the hour. The bathrooms and water closets are ready. My footmen will be complete shortly. You can tell your men they can go up when they are ready. One officer told me they will take shifts patrolling the palace." The Major was pleased with the speed of the staff. "Thank you, sir, the Inspector and I appreciate that. As you see, we have posted officers at the laundry and exit used in the crimes. Please remind the staff they are out of bounds." Lars nodded and assisted the kitchen staff to carry up the evening meal.

Mary was still in Michael's room with Charles and Willem. Willem moved another bed into Michael's room for Charles. "I will lock and barricade the door to Michael's room, only the door from my room will be available." Willem continued over to Charles. "My lord, I request that you always notify me of your movements. And you shall not move from this room without a Royal Guard." Charles nodded and asked, "Will you stay here with Michael?" Willem nodded.

A house maid walked to the door and knocked. Willem walked around and greeted the maid in the hall. "May I help you?" he asked her. "Mevrouw, Fleur sent me to notify the family the evening meal is in the small dining room." Willem guided the maid into Michael's room. "My lady," he said softly, "The house maid has been sent for you to eat your evening meal." Mary turned to Willem and snapped, "I will not leave my son's side!" Willem shuffled the maid out, "You may want to send up food for everyone to this room."

By this time, there had been armed uniform police stationed around in and out of Palace Nassau. They had also been stationing around the grounds of the estate. The one stationed at the main entrance rang the bell as the royal doctor's auto pulled up. A very well-dressed man in a green suit with black-framed glasses and a felt hat stepped out of the car. Two women in nurse's uniforms followed closely behind.

The Royal Police officer at the door stopped the three and requested identification. The doctor handed him his Royal staff credentials, "I am Doctor Arends, and I have been requested by the Prime Minister and sent by Her Majesty Queen Wilhelmina.

The officer assigned to cover the grand entrance opened the door from inside. "This is the doctor," said one officer to the other. The one stepped to the side, allowing the doctor and his nurses to enter. "His lordship is in the grand study; "I will escort you there," the officer announced. The young officer knocked on the large double doors leading into the main study. The doors were opened by the first footman named

Bram. "This is the Royal Physician and his nurses," announced the officer. Bram announced them to Robert and was motioned to enter by the Earl.

"My lord, your cousin, Her Majesty, has directed me to care not only for your son but the entire family in these distressing times." Robert motioned for him to sit in front of his large desk. The two nurses stayed at the double doors. "I am concerned because Michael has not spoken since the incident," said Robert as the doctor sat in the chair. The doctor nodded, "I have seen similar cases in the war, my lord. We are calling it shell shocked." He continued, "We see the soldiers are having similar symptoms after the great war. A great stress to the mind causes them to shut down in a way." Robert stood from his chair. "I will take you to my son now, doctor. My wife, the Marquess of Luxly, and the teacher are in his room now." Robert walked out of his study and instructed one of the uniformed officers to escort them to Michael's room.

The officer knocked on the bedroom door, and Willem answered. Robert stepped Infront of the officer and walked into the room. "I have the doctor with me," Robert said as he walked past Willem. The Inspector was in the room as well to issue Willem with his pistol.

Mary was now sitting in one of the chairs next to the big windows, reading. Charles was sitting next to his friend in bed while reading. "Mary, this is Doctor Arends." Mary walked over to be next to Michael. "Charles has been talking to Michael, but he never responds," Mary said to Doctor Arends. "My son has not responded to questions since the staff rescued him."

"I must be left alone with the young man and my nurses," the doctor demanded. "I will meet with you when I am done assessing him, my lord." Robert took Mary's hand, and they walked out. "We will be in the main study when you are done doctor," he said as they walked through the door. Willem met them at the hall, "I will remain in this room the entire time, my lord." Robert put his free hand on Willem's right shoulder, "Good Man!" Charles was close behind Robert and Mary. A uniformed Royal Police officer escorted them down to the ground floor.

While Robert, Mary, and Charles waited in the grand study, a uniformed policeman came to the door. "My lord, Inspector Jansen requested I notify you of the arrival of additional resources." Robert walked to the officer; they stepped out the entry to find two military trucks followed by several motorcars. Major Dekker and Inspector Jansen walked over to Robert. "My lord, these are the men tasked to finding the culprit. I have requested a special investigator to come as well."

What looked to be twenty-four men in uniform marched into Palace Nassau. The Major directed his men to the second floor. Inspector Jansen directed his men to the basement. The Marechaussee cook and kitchen staff were the last to approach the door. Major Dekker directed them to meet with the head cook in the basement. While Dekker's men set up on the second floor, Jansen had his men set up office and interview rooms in the basement that Lars set up.

Robert was in his study with Mary and Charles. The Prime Minister and the Minister of Defense were also in the study. Robert was talking to Mary about the Marechaussee and the Royal Police arriving when a knock at the study door interrupted him. The first footman opened it to have Lars standing on the other side. "Please ask his lordship to come to the kitchen through the servant's passage," Lars whispered. "Tell him Inspector Jansen and Major Dekker wish to speak with him."

Bram walked over to Robert and relayed Lars' message. Robert took the hidden passage next to the fireplace behind the large bookcase. The Prime Minister and Minister of Defense stood, but Robert held up his hand to stop them. Robert arrived to find Jansen and Dekker waiting for him at the base of the passage. Both bowed and Jansen said, "My lord, I have word from one of your grounds keepers they found the hat and scarf worn by the man they chased." Dekker held up a black wool hat and a black wool scarf. "Please do not touch sir, but have you seen these before?" asked Dekker. "It could be anyone's," Robert replied. "Everyone has something like these, but not in the summer months." Dekker turned them over to expose strands of red hair. "Do you know anyone with red hair, my lord?" asked Dekker. "No, not that I can think of...you remember people with red hair." Jansen placed the cap and scarf into an evidence bag and handed it to a uniformed officer waiting behind him. "We will give this to Brigadier de Groot when he arrives," said Dekker. Robert returned to his study using the hidden passage.

As he stepped in, he found the Prime Minister and Minister of Defense collecting their things. "My lord, we will make our leave for tonight." The two bowed to Robert. "We do not wish to be in the way of the investigation," said the Prime Minister. The Minister of Defense spoke up as he collected his briefcase. "Can you please place this into your safe and review the documents when you are less distracted, my lord?"

Robert took it and walked over to the other side of the fireplace. He pulled the bookcase to expose a very large vault. There are three combination dials and a spinning handle. Robert conceals the dials as he entered the combinations, opened the vault, placed the briefcase inside, and secured it. "I will review them later," Robert said as he pushes the bookcase back.

As the Prime Minister and the Minister of Defense walked out, the Doctor walked into the study. "Doctor Arends" Mary called out. Robert, Mary, and Charles stood up to greet the Doctor. Mary gestured to him to sit next to her on a large sofa. "I am comfortable calling this shell shock," Doctor Arends informed them as he sat next to Mary. He looked to Mary and Robert, "I expect he will recover with the help of his family, but must be made to feel protected and safe. I have a couple of nurses with me, and they will attend to his daily needs."

Right as the doctor finished his statement, Major Dekker walked into the study and bowed. "My lord, I want to introduce to you Brigadier de Groot from Amsterdam. He is the best investigator the Royal Police have." The detective walked in and bowed as he took off his brown felt hat.

"I will do everything in my power to find the culprit,

my lord, and I will need the cooperation of your entire family and staff." The Brigadier continued, "What is this I hear of a missing footman and blood, my lord?"

Brigadier de Groot was a tall and slim man in his late thirties. Robert looked him up and down and found him impeccably dressed and had the manor of a military man. The Brigadier had a neatly maintained beard that he obviously took great pride in. In just a few moments, the Earl Nassau would understand the importance of Brigadier de Groot.

Chapter

7

Robert stood up from his chair and walked over to the two police officials. They both bowed again. There was something different about Robert since his son's incident. His facial expression, posture, and each movement he made were now rigid.

Robert extended his hand to the Brigadier. "You have the full support of the family and my staff. I do not care what you have to do, but you must find the man who harmed my son."

"May I speak to you in private, my lord?" asked the Brigadier.

As Brigadier Johannes de Groot returned his hand to his side, Robert noticed his signet ring. Johannes was awarded The Order of the Lion by Her Majesty two years prior. The Brigadier was awarded the highest civilian order of chivalry, the Knight Grand Cross. His signet ring showed the gold lion on blue enamel in the center of the ring.

Johannes was the detective who solved the worst crimes of the Great War. When it ended in 1918, Johannes was knighted for his solving a mass murder disguised by the war. Her Majesty also declared Johannes the greatest detective in the Kingdom of the Netherlands. His formal title is De hoogwelgeboren heer Johannes ridder de Groot. He, however, does not use his formal title, only his rank with the Rijkspolitie.

The three men walked into the hall outside the study. "I have been made aware of some evidence, my lord. I would like to begin with my investigation of the scene in the laundry, if I may." Robert directed the Major to take him below stairs. The Brigadier turned, "When may I speak with his lordships son?" he asked Robert. "My son is not speaking and is under the care of a physician. You will need to speak with Doctor Arends about that." The Brigadier nodded in understanding and continued to below stairs.

Robert returned to his study and sat next to Mary. "I think we need to reach out to James and Elizabeth Luxly." Charles walked over to Robert and stood Infront of him. "I do not wish to leave, sir; I wish to remain with my friend." Charles looked sad and appeared to be begging, without actually begging, Robert and Mary to allow this. Robert looked at Charles and said, "I wish to ask your parents to arrive sooner than their plans originally allowed. I feel they should be here as well, for Michael's sake. The doctor said we need to make Michael feel safe, and your presence here will do just that. Your parents should be here with you."

With Mary in agreement, she walked over to the bell pull. "I will have Lars send a telegram tonight. They should be able to arrive in a couple of days." Lars entered the room, and Mary gave him his instructions. Once Lars stepped away, the first footman assigned to the study asked, "Shall I ensure the William of Orange room is ready now?" Mary nodded and gave him permission to leave the study. "We have everything here we need for now, Bram. If we need anything, I will ring the bell."

Mary walked back to Robert and took his hands into hers as she sat next to him. "My love, I am worried about you. You do not look or act like yourself." She continued, "You look as if you have become a new person, and it worries me." Robert did not even look up at his wife when he said, "Our only child was almost taken from us today. I do not know why or who, but I cannot allow it to happen again."

Charles was sitting in one of the large chairs next to Robert and Mary. He was thinking about what Mary said was true. "He was always so informal and made everyone feel comfortable, now he is the opposite," Charles thought to himself. Charles was looking at his best friend's father, his Godfather, and noticed something even more strange. "I have never seen him look so angry or scary, but he has the eyes of a man who could kill."

The tall clock standing next to the doors chimed nine o'clock. Charles stood up and requested to be taken up to Michael's room. Mary opened the study doors and motioned to one of the uniformed policemen standing outside. "Please take the Marquess to his room."

The policeman bowed and gestured to Charles. For the first time in his life, Charles turned to Robert and Mary and bowed to them, and then walked out of the room.

As they were walking up the main stairs, the policeman said, "My lord, all of us are wishing you, the family, and the Earl's son well. We promise to protect all of you no matter the cost." Charles shook the policeman's hand, thanked him, and knocked on the door.

Willem opened it and allowed Charles to enter. "I am stepping into the hall just outside the bedroom door, my lord, but will return shortly," Willem said to Charles.

While Willem was speaking to the police officials in the hall, Charles changed into his pajamas and dressing gown. He opened the door and said, "I need the water closet, please." The policeman talking to Willem walked him down the hall and stood outside the door. Once completed, walked him back to the bedroom. "Willem, I am going to sleep. has Michael said anything yet?"

"No, my lord, but he is sleeping now." Charles checked on his friend, walked around the bed, and climbed in next to him.

Willem kept his word and had not left his post. He has set up the room connected to Michael's as his own. As he collected some items, he grabbed the keys and stepped into the hall. Locking the door behind him, "Officer, can you please guard the door. I am going to the water closet for a few minutes." A uniformed Royal Policeman walked over and stood in Infront of the door.

Willem arrived only five minutes later and returned to find the same officer guarding the door to his room. "Thank you," Willem stated as he removed the keys from his pocket. "I will attempt to sleep now, and I will lock the door behind me. Please remain in the main hallway." The officer nodded and told Willem they would have a shift change in an hour. "I will inform the next shift as well, sir."

Willem locked the door, leaving the key fully turned inside the lock. Some light was coming from Michael's room. As he walked through the small passage connecting the rooms, he noticed Charles in bed, reading with the bedside light on. "Oh!" Willem was surprised to see the Marquess still awake. "I could not sleep, so I decided to read some," replied Charles.

"I am going to try to sleep. Please wake me if you need to leave for any reason or need me. Please do not let yourself out." Charles nodded in understanding and returned to his reading. Willem took his pistol and placed it inside the bedside table. After climbing into bed and pulling up the covers, he fell asleep quickly.

Below stairs, Brigadier de Groot placed his briefcase on the table in the old cook's rooms. As he was pulling out supplies, he cleared his throat. "Lars, I understand you have been the butler to the family for many years."

"Yes, sir, I have been on the estate since I was just 20

years of age," replied Lars. "Excellent! I need a list of every staff member of the estate; can you provide it?" asked de Groot. Lars reached into his right-hand jacket pocket and pulled out a paper folded in half. "Here, sir, I had expected this request." Lars handed it over to de Groot with a smile. Lars continued, "I have included the length of employment, their role, if they live in the house or cottage, and the ones who live off the estate, I have included their address." Lars looked up at the Brigadier to see him smile slightly. "Well, my good man, you are very detailed. I expect your position here requires you to expect other people's needs."

"I take great pride in that, sir," replied Lars.

The Brigadier set the paper on the table. "I will need to interview everyone in the household and the staff who work the grounds. In the morning, I will provide you a schedule. Can you make sure they arrive on time?" Lars nodded. "I will suggest you meet the house staff first, sir. The groundskeepers work rather early, harvesting and other farming chores. The house staff will be easier to arrange first," de Groot nodded. "That will work nicely, thank you. I would like to meet with your first thing in the morning if you do not object." Lars stood up straighter, "I would be most happy to, sir, anything for this family." Lars turned and walked away.

The Brigadier opened the paper Lars gave him. "A nicely typed and organized list, he thought to himself. Then he sighed, "Twenty-two house staff and fifteen grounds staff." He started planning a timeline for the thirty-seven staff interviews. As he was writing these down, the Inspector walked in. "Hallo, my friend, thank you for coming so quickly." The Brigadier stood and saluted his friend. "Now-now Johannes, no need for the formality."

The two sat down at the table, and de Groot slid the list of staff over to the Inspector."Well! It looks like we have our list of suspects here. Not a short one I am sorry to say," Jan commented. "What makes you think the suspect is on that list?" asked Johannes. Jan leaned forward as he pushed the list back to his friend. "For the same reason you do." Jan sat back in the chair. "This is an inside job. The door Michael was carried out from is hidden, and only staff or family would know. Then there is the blood in the laundry with the knife.

AND there is still the missing footman to rule out." Johannes sighed, slumping into the chair further. "I wanted you to look at the laundry with me. I see you have a man stationed there." The two stood up and walked down the hallway toward the laundry. Johannes held his hand up, stopping the two halfway. "I am not sure that the missing footman is related, and I am not convinced that he is a suspect.

Something is telling me that the blood may be related to him." Just as Johannes finished his statement, Major Dekker walked up to them. "Are you going to the laundry?" asked Dekker. The two nodded, and the three continued down the hall. The uniformed policeman was sat in a chair, blocking the closed door. As the three made their approach, the officer stood and handed the Brigadier the key.

"No one has been in or out, sir, no one has even walked down the hall," asserted the officer. As the three men walked into the laundry, the blood was very well dried. Brigadier de Groot scanned the large room and stopped when he saw the bloodied kitchen knife. "I will add this to the safe where I have the cap and scarf," de Groot said as he picked it up.

The Brigadier was wearing brown leather gloves and placed the knife into an envelope. "I have already had my men check for fingermarks, but I am told there are several.

Not surprising being the laundry for the palace," Major Dekker announced. The Brigadier turned and asked if they had checked the knife, and Dekker assured him they had. "Have we confirmed this knife came from the kitchens here?" asked de Groot. Neither the Inspector nor the Major could answer that question.

Johannes stepped out and ordered the policeman to get the cook or a kitchen maid. A few minutes later, Cornelia arrived. "How may I help?" she asked. "Mevrouw, I understand you are the head cook for the palace. Can you tell me if this knife belongs to your kitchens?" Johannes held up the bloodied knife for Cornelia to see. The policeman had to act quickly to catch the cook as she fainted from the sight of it.

The Major attended to his old friend while the Inspector looked for staff to assist. Johannes thought to himself, "I can take her off the suspects list, I think. She cannot even handle the sight of blood." He placed the knife back into the envelope and placed it into his briefcase.

Lars and Fleur walked toward Cornelia with the Inspector behind them. "Please attend to her," barked Johannes. The Major looked toward him and glared at him with disapproval. "I did not expect the woman to faint," replied de Groot. The Brigadier walked back into the laundry, scanning around again.

From inside the laundry, de Groot called out to the policeman in the hall. The man walked in and quickly back out. He had been tasked with looking at all the kitchen knives to see if they were a match.

"It is getting late," said Inspector Jansen. The Major agreed, and the two walked down the hall to the old cook's rooms. The Major, the Inspector, and the Brigadier would stay in these rooms. There were extra beds brought, so the one room now had three beds. In the corner was a large vault. Extra uniforms were brought for the men, which were hanging on the wardrobe on the opposite side of the room. Johannes pulled the laundry door closed and locked it. After handing the policeman the key, he mumbled something, the officer could not understand. The well-dressed man looked tired walking down the hall. The policeman stopped the Brigadier halfway down the hall. "It matches the knives in the kitchen, sir."

Once Johannes walked into the old cook's rooms, he walked into the bedroom. "I will lock this up with the others," he said as he turned the key in the lock. He placed the envelope with the knife next to the cap and scarf. After closing and locking it, he turned to his colleagues. "I dislike kidnapping cases. I dislike murder cases. Give me burglary cases any day." The

three discussed their plans for the following day and
went to sleep.

Chapter
8

At five o'clock Johannes woke up and walked into the connecting sitting room. He was holding the list of staff that Lars provided him, carefully reading each name with their role in the palace.

Once he made it to the head cook, he wrote, "Faints at the sight of blood" in pencil next to her name. He noted that she lives in a cottage on the estate with her sister. The Major and the Inspector walked into the sitting room to find Johannes with a frown on his face and his eyes squinched in deep thought. "My friend, you have always been too serious. You always solve the case. What is causing you this discomfort?" asked the Inspector. Without looking up, Johannes spoke softly. "There are so many possibilities here." The Major spoke up as he sat next to the investigator. "So, you do think it is an inside job?" I did not say that." Johannes quickly replied with a tone of disapproval. "I am just saying there are so many possibilities in this case."

"After eating something, I want to be shown the missing footman's rooms," said Johannes. The three walked to the kitchens after locking the door behind them. Two military cooks and several uniformed police officers met them.

One of the police officers approached the Inspector. "We are taking our morning meal now, and then the Major's men will come down." Both the Inspector and the Major nodded. "I shall take my morning meal and coffee with me," said Johannes as he left the kitchens.

Johannes unlocked the door and sat at the table in the sitting area. He was making mental notes to search the footman's rooms and then to have the butler schedule the interviews when his thoughts were interrupted by a knock at the door. As he turned to look, he was a uniformed policeman standing next to the young Marquess.

"My lord," Johannes said with a questioning tone to his voice. "What are you doing down here, sir?" Charles, still in his pajamas and dressing gown, stepped into the room. As the policeman informed the Brigadier that Charles had insisted he see him first thing. Johannes held up his hand and nodded in understanding. Charles turned and closed the door in the policeman's face. "I want to talk to you in private, Brigadier de Groot." The Brigadier gestured to the chair next to him. "I cannot offer you tea, my lord," Johannes said as he sat back down. "What do you wish to speak to me about, my lord?" Charles sat next to the Brigadier and stared at him for a moment before speaking.

"Michael and I have explored every room, hall, passage, and staircase since I arrived. The Earl Nassau gave us permission to search the staff areas after the footman, Antoon, went missing. Michael and I went into Antoon's bedroom alone and found this." Charles pulled a worn leather wallet out of his dressing gown pocket. "I wanted to make sure someone of importance saw this." The Brigadier opened it to see some Dutch guilders and British pounds.

"What about this made you feel it important?? He held the wallet up to examine it. "Brigadier, look inside the wallet." Johannes pulled out a piece of torn paper with some handwriting on it. He turned over the scrap to find the words "Koninklijke Marechaussee" written in pencil. Johannes suddenly felt ill and intrigued at the same time. Charles pointed and said, "I snuck back up to the footman's room after… and took it. I remember seeing the Marechaussee written, and I did not know what it was. I was sitting on the wallet on the bedside table. Once the Koninklijke Marechaussee arrived here yesterday, I knew I needed to protect it." Johannes stood hastily, causing the chair he was sitting on to crash against the wall. The uniformed police officer in the hallway pushed the door open. "Whatever is the matter in here?"

"Get the butler in here as well as the Inspector and the Major….immediately!" shouted Johannes. The Brigadier looked down at the young Marquess, "I want you to take us up to Antoon's rooms." Charles nodded in agreement. A few moments later, Lars and the others arrived as instructed. Johannes instructed the police officer to stand guard of the old cook's rooms. "Lars, take us to Antoon's rooms immediately," Johannes stated with a tone of excitement in his voice. "My dear friend, whatever has come over you?" Johannes' manner astonished the Inspector. "The young Marquess may have saved some interesting evidence." Johannes handed the wallet with the torn paper exposed to the Inspector. The Major spoke up, "My lord, you found this in the footman's rooms?" Charles only nodded. Lars let the group into the men's section of the staff apartments.

After opening the door leading to Antoon's rooms, Johannes spoke, "Please stay here Lars." Johannes guided Charles into the rooms, "Show us, my lord." Charles walked the men through the small sitting room into the adjoining bedroom. Charles pointed over to the bedside table. "It was just lying there sir…." His voice faded as his gaze turned to the bed. Charles had a look that worried the men. The Major asked, "What is the matter, my lord? What do you see?" Charles pointed to the now-empty bed. "Antoon's clothing was laid out neatly there just yesterday.

They were there when I came to get the wallet." Brigadier turned to Charles, "My lord, thank you for coming forward with this information and brining me the wallet. Please leave us to this, and I will talk with you later."

"I will take him down to his room, gentlemen," said Lars from the hallway. The Inspector spoke up quickly, "I am sorry, sir, but that will not do. I will take his lordship down to his room." To the Major and Brigadier, he said, "I will return, gentlemen," and left the rooms with Charles.

As they walked down the servant's staircase, the Inspector asked, "How did you gain access to this area or even the footman's rooms?" At the bottom of the stairs, Charles turned to him. "The Earl Nassau gave Michael and I permission to search ALL areas. I took the hidden passage up, and the door was open. That is also part of the reason I felt I needed to protect the wallet." The Inspector nodded and handed the young Marquess off to Willem. The Inspector returned using the servants' staircase. Once he was in Antoon's rooms, he informed them of the information he got from the Marquess. The Brigadier and the Major sighed from the chairs upon which they sat in the sitting room. The Inspector took out a cigarette and offered his colleagues one.

After lighting his, the Inspector shook his head with confusion. "What does all of this mean?" he asked. The men spoke a few minutes while they smoked, then the Brigadier snuffed out the rest of his cigarette and walked into the bedroom once again. Taking out a small notebook and pen, he started writing down an inventory of the room. He opened each drawer of the chest of drawers and the bedside table, then looked under the bed. He pulled off all the bed linen and lifted the mattress. Once completed in there, he walked into the sitting room and began the same process there. "I am done here; I must go down and think," he muttered. The three went into their temporary quarters. Johannes opened the safe and placed the wallet into it, and then locked it again. He quickly walked through the sitting room and into the office area.

A uniformed policeman was sitting at a desk. "I need you to take some notes for me," said Johannes. The policeman grabbed a notepad and pencil, took down what the Brigadier said, and walked out. "What was that all about?" asked the Major. "I have changed the order of the interviews," replied Johannes. He continued, "I gave Lars a schedule. This changes that schedule."

"Oh?" exclaimed the Major. "How so, my friend?" asked the Inspector. "I want to interview the male house staff first, starting with the butler." The Inspector and Major nodded in sequence, now thinking the missing footman may be related to the blood in the laundry. "I have also sent him to get as much background on Antoon from the Rijkspolitie records and the Koninklijke Marechaussee." The Inspector looked at the two and asked openly, "Could Antoon be one of us?" Johannes shook his head in disagreement, "I do not think he is one of us, but I think he may have tried to contact the Marechaussee. But I cannot think why." He went back to the safe and collected the evidence they had so far. Lars walked down the hall to the old cook's rooms, being led by the uniformed policeman. At the end of the hall lined with wooden chairs placed there earlier, the policeman turned and knocked on the door. "Come in," said the Brigadier.

Lars was directed through to the old cook's sitting room. A large table was placed to the side of the room and lined with four chairs. "Please sit, Lars," said the Major, directing him to the chair next to his. At the end of the table was a uniformed policeman from the Rijkspolitie holding a notebook and pencil.

The Inspector sat down, followed by the Brigadier. Johannes pulled out a small piece of paper and a pen. He handed it to Lars and instructed him to write his full name, his date of birth, and place of birth. "Please sign your name at the bottom when you are finished," said Johannes.

Lars followed the instructions given to him, signed his name, and slid the paper and pen back to the Brigadier. Johannes passed the paper off to the Rijkspolitie officer at the end of the table. The policeman took the sheet of paper as Johannes began his questioning.

"Thank you, Lars, for taking the time out of your busy schedule to meet with us."

The Brigadier continued, "You understand how important this process is."

Lars adjusted his suit jacket and quickly replied, "I do, sir."

"The officer will take notes as we ask you questions.

Please speak clearly and plainly."

"I see you have been working for the Nassau family for several years."

"Yes sir, I came to Palace Nassau as a footman when I was just twenty years of age. Next month will make it thirty years."

"When did you hire the missing footman, Antoon?"

"He came to us five years ago. He came from The Hague after being hired at the Noordeinde Palace."

"Why did he not work at Noordeinde Palace?"

"The head butler of Noordeinde Palace interviewed him to fill the position here."

"Is that common practice?"

"Yes, Brigadier, all staff for the Palace Nassau are hired through Her Majesty's Government. They are paid through the Palace Nassau's income, but are hired through Her Majesty. This is the residence of the sitting Earl Nassau, and so it is considered a royal position."

"Do you have access to his references or a list of his previous employers?"

"I thought you would want that information." Lars pulled out four pieces of paper that had been folded as if they came from an envelope. "Here you are, sir, I have four letters from previous employers."

"Do you have similar information for the other staff?"

"Only for the male staff, sir, you will have to obtain the female staff information from the head housekeeper." The Brigadier pulled out the piece of torn paper from Antoon's wallet and held it up for Lars to see. "Is this Antoon's handwriting?"

Lars leaned forward and put on his glasses. "It appears to be, sir. What is it?"

"We do not quite know as of yet. The young Marquess of Luxly found it in Antoon's rooms." The Inspector spoke up, "Speaking of, were you aware that Antoon's rooms were left unlocked?"

"Yes, I left it unlocked after we found that he was missing, and I let the Earl, Meneer Michael, and the young Marquess into the rooms." Lars sighed, "Was that a mistake?" The Brigadier shrugged. "You found Antoon to be responsible?"

"Very! I counted on him more than any other house staff."

"Then why was he the second footman and not the first?" Lars looked uncomfortable, shifted in his chair, and thought for a moment. "That decision was not mine to make. He was hired to fill the position of second footman. It was not long for him to gain my trust."

"Do you not like the first footman?"

"It is not like that sir; I like Bram, and he works hard. One could even go as far as saying he is proud to work for the Nassau's. I just find Antoon reminds me of my late brother."

"Could your feelings be blinding your opinion of Antoon?"

"Not at all; I put the family first and would let nothing disrupt the protocol of things."

"What first alerted you to Antoon's absence?"

"The first and second footmen may start thirty minutes

later than the others. The third, fourth, and fifth footmen come to the kitchens at five o" clock. At six o'clock, Bram came to my office to alert me to Antoon's absence."

"What are Antoon's duties?"

"He has a wide range of duties. The first and second footmen function as my primary assistants.

They help me attend to the family directly and maintain the daily function of the household. They are also in charge of making sure the meals are served properly and in a timely manner."

"How has the new household staff settled in?"

Lars again thought for a moment before he answered. "I know Emma was assigned to the Earl Nassau shortly before their moving in. Tess was assigned to the Countess Nassau while they still lived in London to help the transition. Willem was assigned to Meneer Michael the month prior, but he came to the palace to set up the classroom about two weeks before their arrival. The only other new staff member is the Countess' lady's maid. But I do not have jurisdiction over any of them."

"What do you mean, you do not have jurisdiction over them?"

"Just that! They are not exactly house staff, but they are not family. They are able to eat with the family or be in the private areas of the palace. But they only report directly to the Earl and Countess Nassau."

"Does that cause problems with the other staff?"

"No, that is standard protocol for households like this."

"Do they live in the house?" The Brigadier shuffled around some papers. He was looking for the list that Lars provided him earlier."

"Willem has a house in Delft, I believe. Emma lives in one of the estate cottages, as does Tess. Emma and Tess are on either side of the cottage, occupied by the head cook and the head housekeeper. But the Countess' lady's maid lives in the house."

"I understand Willem has been asked by his lordship to move into the palace. He is now the bodyguard." The Brigadier found the list. "You also live in a cottage, I see."

"That is correct, Brigadier, I moved into it when I became butler."

"Where were you when Meneer Michael was taken?"

Lars sat up even straighter. "I followed the Earl Nassau to below stairs when the Marquess announced that he and Meneer Michael found a knife and some blood in the laundry."

"What time what that, Lars?"

"It was exactly eleven fifty, sir. I looked at the mantel clock when the Marquess walked into the Delft porcelain room. I was reviewing some of the inventory of the Delft porcelain with the Earl and Countess when the young Marquess announced the finding."

"How did you go about finding Meneer Michael?"

"We could hear some shouting outdoors after finding……"

The Brigadier held up his hand and nodded. "Please continue."

"We went out the door outside of the laundry to see the outdoor staff chasing someone. The head groundskeeper was holding the young man up and talking to him."

"What time do you think it was when you went outdoors?"

"We were only in the laundry for a few minutes. I looked at my watch as his lordship walked Meneer Michael up to the house. We arrived at the large study at twelve ten. So, possibly twelve o'clock was when we walked out."

"Do you have any opinion of what happened to the missing Antoon?" Lars only shook his head. "Do you think it is possible that Antoon has something to do with the attempted kidnapping of Meneer Michael? Lars only shook his head again. "Do you think that another palace staff member could be involved?"

Lars looked shaken by that idea. "I certainly hope not and cannot see a reason anyone in the palace would do such a thing!"

"I am not used to an aristocrat including their son in such a manner as he does. Would you say that the Earl Nassau is close to Meneer Michael?"

"Exactly!" Lars nodded. "The Earl and Countess Nassau were both raised by aristocratic parents, quite at arm's length. His lordship especially wants his son to have a better relationship than what he had with the late Earl. Also, I may add that I feel his lordship wishes his son will be better prepared to inherit the Palace and title than he was."

"I would like to ask if you recognize any of these," the Brigadier asked as he placed the woollen cap and scarf on the table before him.

"May I?" Asked Lars as he reached for the items. "Please do not touch them." Lars leaned forward again to get a look. "Looks like what anyone would have during the winter months."

"So, you could not say for sure who they belonged to?"

"Definitely not, I am afraid."

"There are strands of red hair inside the cap. Are there any red-haired staff on the estate? Do you know of any red-haired people even?"

"No, sir, there are no red-haired staff here. I have only seen some red-haired people on my travels." The Brigadier sat back in his chair, "I have nothing else for you at this time. I ask that you be available for any further questioning. That is, if my colleagues have nothing to ask." The Brigadier looked to the Inspector and the Major, both of whom were shaking their heads no in response.

"Did you get everything written down, officer? The Brigadier asked while looking to the end of the table.

"I did, sir," replied the officer assigned to taking notes. The Brigadier stood and thanked Lars for his time. "Can you please ask the footmen to come down?" Lars turned and said, "I cannot leave the family without footmen. May I send two at a time?" The Brigadier nodded and replied with, "Send down the two you can spare first. I wish to speak with Bram last." Lars did a small bow out of respect to the policemen and walked out the door.

The Inspector stood and walked over to get himself some tea. As he held up the kettle in an offering the tea to the others, they nodded. "I have to say, we could use some men like Lars in the Rijkspolitie," said the Inspector. "Absolutely!" agreed the Major, "As could we."

"What do you think about our missing Antoon?" asked the Major. The Brigadier did not respond. He continued to just look forward, rubbing his dark beard. "He rubs that beard like he is tuning in a radio," said the Inspector to the Major. "As long as he gets a clear signal," said the Major, laughing and taking the cup of tea from the Inspector.

As the Inspector placed a cup of tea in front of the Brigadier, he could hear his friend speaking just below his breath. He was now scratching his beard and mumbling. "Must be static," joked the Inspector, looking at the Major. Johannes stood and carried his tea over to the group of chairs the others sat down in. "Something is telling me that our missing Antoon is a victim and not a suspect." The Inspector and Major looked to the Brigadier to explain further. "I just feel like we are going to find a body somewhere, and this will end up being a murder and an attempted kidnapping."

The Major leaned forward. "I think we should interview the Earl gently and with her ladyship present." The others nodded in agreement. "I think we should do their interviews after the evening meal. I will send up a message to the Earl with Lars," continued the Major. The three interviewed the other footmen, and there was just Bram left to interview. The previous footmen provided nothing important, being they were providing the same information about Antoon as Lars did. Antoon was well-liked by the others, apparently.

Chapter

9

As the fifth footman walked out, Bram de Vries knocked on the door. The Major gestured to the first footman to sit next to him at the table. Bram de Vries was the look of a first footman. His dark hair was neatly placed, freshly shaven, high, crisp white collar, black tie perfectly tied, and the black suit appeared to have been custom-made for him. As he walked over to the table, the Major looked down to his shoes to see they were perfectly polished.

Bram gave a courtesy bow to the men and sat where he was directed. "I have been instructed to give this to you, Brigadier." He handed him a sealed envelope with "Bram de Vries–First Footman" written on the front. As the Brigadier opened the envelope, he instructed Bram to write his full name, date of birth, place of birth, and to sign his name at the bottom. "Ah, your butler is very organized," said the Brigadier to Bram.

The Brigadier pulled out four letters of reference

related to Bram's previous employment. "I see you were fifth and fourth footman at Dam Palace before being assigned here as second footman." Bram nodded in response. "You also served in the Royal Military, I see." Bram again only nodded.

"Nothing to be ashamed about serving in the war," said the Brigadier. Bram, still looking at him, replied, "I am not ashamed, just was drafted, sir. I was not a career soldier." Johannes was now the one nodding in understanding and began his questioning. "Do you enjoy working for the Nassau family?" "Very much, sir. The late Earl Nassau was not the easiest to work for, but he was kind. The late Earl paid well, and the new Earl gave me a small raise to stay on."

"What is your opinion about Antoon?"

Bram sighed slightly, "I like him very much, sir. He and I spend our off times together, mostly. We have similar interests, and the previous second footman stayed in his rooms, mostly."

"Does Antoon have a lady in his life?"

"He has never mentioned one to me. We are here mostly. He may have in Delft."

"Delft?"

"His mother lives in Gouda, but he also goes to Delft on some of his off days, so he may have a lady friend in Delft."

"Do you ever go to Gouda or Delft with Antoon?"

"No, sir, if I go out on my off days, I go to Breda to visit family."

"I see you live in the palace; your rooms are next to Antoon's, I understand."

"Correct, sir."

"When did you see Antoon last?"

"The evening before his disappearance. We had finished the evening meals for the family, and we were cleaning up the dining room."

"What does Antoon usually do before going to his rooms for the evening?"

"Most of us stay up in the staff sitting room outside our dining room, relaxing. He was there that evening, but I went up to my rooms earlier than normal that night."

"Why?"

"I was not feeling the best that night, had congestion and was more tired than usual."

"Did you notice anything different about Antoon or the other staff?"

"No, that night I was awoken by the sound of Antoon falling into bed late, but I went back to sleep."

"Do you know what time that was?"

"I am afraid not, Brigadier, I was not feeling well and went back to sleep immediately."

"On a normal day, what time do you wake up?"

"I normally wake up at four thirty. That allows me first chance to the bathroom and water closet."

"Do you know what time Antoon usually wakes up?"

"Around the same time as I do, sir. He usually uses the facilities after me."

"When did you first realize that Antoon was missing?"

"It was somewhere around six o'clock, I think. The other footmen had their chores completed, and I went to find Antoon. I went and told the butler around that time."

"Do you think Antoon could be associated with the attempted?"

Bram interrupted the Brigadier, "Absolutely not! There is absolutely no possibility that Antoon could be associated with Meneer Michael's kidnapping."

Johannes was taken by this interruption. He sat back slightly more in his chair. "Do you feel that any of the staff could be associated with the kidnapping attempt?" Bram shook his head.

"Where were you when the attempted kidnapping was taking place?"

"I was in the silver vault polishing, sir."

"Where is the silver vault?"

"It is on the opposite side of the basement, sir. I never heard the commotion."

"When did you find out about the attempt?"

"The butler pulled the bell cord in the large study around twelve thirty. The third footman and I went up and was told to lock the palace down."

Bram repositioned himself slightly. "May I ask a question, gentleman?" The three nodded. "Could this be related to the Earl Nassau's position in Her Majesty's government? The Prime Minister has spent many hours here."

The Inspector spoke up first. "That is an option, but we have nothing as of yet."

"Do you know Antoon's handwriting?" The Brigadier prepared to pull out the torn paper.

"I do not think I do, sir."

"Do you know this handwriting?" The Brigadier asked as he held up the torn paper. "No, sir."

"Do you recognize these?" The Brigadier placed the cap and scarf onto the table.

Bram looked and replied, "Looks like they could be anyone's, but who would wear them in the summer months?"

"The man who attempted to kidnap Meneer Michael."

"OH!"

"Do you know anyone with red hair?"

Bram thought for a moment. "No, sir, you do not see

many red-haired people around here."

"Would you say the relationship the Earl Nassau has with his son is unusually close?"

"You mean for a man of his title and position?" The Brigadier nodded.

"I would say he is providing a better life than he had when he was a child here."

"Oh?"

"It is my understanding that the Earl Nassau was not close to the late Earl. I believe he left here when he was twenty or so to attend university in London."

"It is my understanding that Meneer Michael has not spoken since his rescue. Have you seen him since he has been in his room?"

"No, sir, Willem is keeping the doors closed and locked at all times. His lordship has tasked him with protecting the boy."

"Who is bringing his meals?"

"Normally it would be myself or Antoon, but there are nurses here now. It is my understanding that Meneer Michael has not ate or drank anything yet."

"What do you know of Willem?"

"I understand he was a teacher for the royal family, but was assigned here when the current Earl inherited."

"Do you interact with Willem much?"

"No, sir, he is not exactly house staff but not family either. He and the secretaries and lady's maid are separate from us."

"Do you ever go into the laundry?"

"Only to drop off table linen or my linen to be cleaned."

"When was the last time you were in the laundry?"

Bram thought for a while, then replied, "A week ago when I took my linen down."

"Do you know who was in the laundry last?"

"I do not, last evenings table linen is still in the pantry between the two dining rooms."

"Does the linen from the estate cottages come to the laundry here?"

"No, sir, they do their own linen in the cottages."

"Would you be opposed to us searching your rooms?"

"Not at all," Bram stated as he pulled out his keys and handed them to the Brigadier.

Johannes motioned to one of the uniformed police officers standing by the door. "Please search the rooms and write a detailed inventory. But please keep it tidy for the gentleman," said the Brigadier.

"Thank you Meneer de Vries. Once the officer completes the search, I will allow you to leave."

"Not a problem, sir, I understand the importance and need of the situation."

"You asked if this could be related to the Earl Nassau's position. What made you think about that?"

"Well, sir, he is the son of the late Defense Minister, he is the Earl Nassau, the cousin to Queen Wilhelmina, and the personal secretary to the Prime Minister. Sounds like a way to ask for ransom money, possibly."

"We have not found a demand for money; usually, they would leave that somewhere to be found. I guess they could have taken the boy, then brought the ransom after, but were unsuccessful." The Brigadier thought for a moment, but that did not feel right to him. "I just have one last question for you, Bram. Do you know why Antoon would have British pound notes in his wallet?"

"Yes, sir, Antoon was sent to London to help with the transition. He was with the family for a week before they traveled here." The police officer returned and handed the keys to Bram. He turned to the Brigadier and handed a notebook with the detailed inventory. Johannes read the officer's notes and then closed the notebook.

"Please be available for further questioning later, and there will be a man taking the staff's fingermarks later." Bram stood and gave another slight bow as he replaced his keys in his pocket.

As Bram stepped out of the room, the Major spoke up. "I think he gave us better information than Lars." The Inspector nodded in agreement and the Brigadier stood. As he walked over to the kettle, he shook it and announced, "Empty." The Inspector took the kettle from the investigator and went to get more tea.

The Major and the Brigadier sat next to each other in the sitting room. The Brigadier reviewing the notes from the interviews they had so far. "I wonder," he said to himself. He was reviewing Bram's interview notes and thought more about this case being connected to the Earl's position. He wrote a quick note in pencil, "Related to the Earl's position?"

Just as he finished his note, the Inspector walked in with coffee and tea. "I brought both," the Inspector stated while holding up both pots. As he poured himself coffee, he stopped mid-pour. "Does the new Earl and family have anything to do with any of this? Or is it even related to the family?" He turned to the Brigadier, holding up the coffee to offer him some.

Johannes nodded to the coffee and replied, "I do not think ransom is involved, but I am thinking it is related to the Earl's position. I do not know why, but this does not feel like it is about money to me." The Major reached up to take the cup of tea and cleared his throat. "You have never been one to explain your feelings, or how you come to your conclusions, but I must ask why you do not think it is about money," demanding the Major.

Inspector Jansen sat next to his colleagues and said, "Johannes, I think you should at least tell us something." The Brigadier shifted a little. "If it is ransom related, I would expect a demand letter just before the kidnapping or at the time of the attempt.

This is a palace; the culprit would not want to take a second risk of returning to leave the demand letter." The Brigadier rubbed his beard again and finished with his thought. "I feel that if they were successful, they would have killed Meneer Michael." A long sigh came from Johannes.

As he looked away from his colleagues, he muttered, "It is time we meet with the Earl and Countess Nassau.

Chapter

10

The three had interviewed all day and into the night. They ate their evening meals in their temporary quarters and came up with a plan for the following day.

"I will send word to the Prime Minister first thing that we need to meet with the Earl and Countess," said Johannes. "Do you think his lordship is awake now?" asked the Major as Lars stepped to their door. "His lordship is in his study; shall I send a message?" asked Lars. The Brigadier wrote a brief message on notepaper and handed it to Lars. "I wanted to mention that I think I know what the scrap paper is that was found in Antoon's wallet," mentioned Lars.

All three of them sat up with intrigue. Lars pulled out a blank piece of stationery from his suit pocket and handed it to Johannes. "This is one stationery papers we have for staff to send letters. It looks to be the same paper to me." The Brigadier sent the Inspector to the safe to collect the paper from the wallet. The three placed the torn paper with "Koninklijke Marechaussee" written on it next to the stationery provided. The Brigadier nodded and whispered, "He was mailing the Koninklijke Marechaussee, but why?" Johannes walked into the connecting office and closed the door behind him. "Lars, please take that message to his lordship, and ask what time will be best for him," said the Inspector. Lars bowed and walked to the large study.

Dekker walked over to the connecting office and attempted to open it. "Locked!" He knocked on the door, "Johannes!" After several moments, Johannes opened the door and walked through to place the evidence back into the safe. "My Good Man!" exclaimed the Inspector. Johannes returned and sat next to his colleagues. "I think our missing footman was attempting to contact the Koninklijke Marechaussee, for some reason." Dekker leaned forward. "The reason would have to be a royal one, or he would write the Rijkspolitie instead."

The fourth footman arrived and collected the dirty dishes. As he walked out, Dekker spoke up and asked, "Is all of this related to the family or is this because of their role in government?" Dekker held up the blank paper provided by Lars. "This could mean it is because of their role in government, and he is a victim." There was no reply from the Inspector or the Brigadier. Then Johannes spoke up, "I wonder if the kidnapping of Meneer Michael was planned or incidental? "Do you think Michael saw something, or do you think……"

Johannes faded off. Lars knocked and said without waiting, "The Earl said to be in the main study at eleven thirty." The Brigadier turned to Lars. "Thank you, sir. I have an additional question for you." Lars stepped into the room and stood in front of the sitting Brigadier. "Please ask your question, sir," said Lars. "Do you have any reason to believe that Antoon has any relations or connection to the Koninklijke Marechaussee?" The Brigadier asked this, looking for any kind of negative response from Lars.

Without thinking, Lars replied, "I have no reason to believe that Antoon has a relation with or any connections with Koninklijke Marechaussee." Lars held up a hand and continued, "You must think he was writing the Koninklijke Marechaussee for some reason, something in the palace must have triggered concern by Antoon, is that right?" The Brigadier stood, and he nodded. Lars simply turned and walked out.

The following morning, the three police officials woke earlier than normal. As they walked to the kitchens, they saw the fourth and fifth footmen completing their tasks in the staff dining room. Brigadier Johannes spoke up, "It is like clockwork in House Nassau." The Inspector nodded. "Just as Bram and Lars mentioned," he agreed as he looked at his watch.

The Marechaussee cooks and kitchen staff were busy preparing the morning meals for the policemen currently stationed at the palace. Johannes collected three coffee cups and walked over to the small sitting area in the second kitchen. Major Dekker and Inspector Jansen were sitting down, reviewing their notebooks.

As Johannes sat down, he said, "I hope the two of you are in agreement that this meeting with the Earl and Countess must be handled with extreme care." The two colleagues nodded in agreement. "I hope that the Prime Minister and Minister of Defense can be in attendance," replied Dekker.

After eating their Dutch pancakes and drinking their coffee, the three stood to walk back to their temporary quarters. "Gentleman," Bram stated as he walked over. "I wanted to let the three of you know that the Duke and Duchess of Luxly will arrive today. They are the parents of the Marquess of Luxly and the closest friends of the Earl and Countess Nassau."

"Thank you," Johannes spoke first. "Do you know what staff they will arrive with?" As Bram nodded, he handed Johannes a telegram from the Luxly's. Johannes read it briefly to see that the Duke and Duchess would arrive with a valet and lady's maid at two o'clock, which Johannes announced to everyone.

Dekker and Jansen went to the young Michael's room on the first floor. After a quick knock on Willem's door, he answered. Willem was in his sleeping clothes and dressing gown. "Morning, gentlemen. How may I help you?" asked Willem. Dekker asked, "Are you aware that the Marquess' parents will arrive today at two o'clock?" Willem nodded and directed the two men into the room. Quietly, the three walked through the small passage connecting the two rooms and into Michael's room. Willem pointed at the bed. "The young Marquess is a dedicated best friend." Charles was asleep next to Michael in the large bed. Dekker placed his hand on Willem's shoulder. "My friend, please feel free to get ready for the day. Inspector Jansen and I will remain with the two young men while you freshen up."

"Thank you, sir!" Willem replied quickly. As Willem collected his change of clothes and walked to the hall, Dekker and Jansen began looking around Michael's room. Jansen had the notebook Charles and Michael used to make the maps.

Quietly, the two men walked around the room occupied by Willem and Michael. They located the hidden passages easily, using the maps drawn by the best friends. Inspector Jansen whispered, "Stay here a moment" as he walked into the hidden passage in Michael's room.

Jansen walked down to the door leading to the Earl's study and then up to the second floor. Jansen returned to Michael's room, and they repeated the action from Willem's room. Willem returned, and Major Dekker turned to him. "We are going to meet with the Earl and Countess this morning at eleven thirty. We have requested the Minister of Defense and the Prime Minister to attend. The Brigadier would like to meet with you once the Duke and Duchess arrive." Willem agreed and locked the bedroom door behind them. Lars arrived at the police command room in the old cook's rooms at eleven o'clock. After knocking on the door, Johannes opened it and greeted Lars. Lars had tea with him on a tray for the three policemen. "May I speak with you before I take you to his lordship's study?" Johannes motioned for Lars to enter and to sit. Instead, Lars began pouring tea for the three as he spoke. "I have been thinking about the situation here, and I could not sleep last night. I cannot help but think that there are secrets in the shadows of House Nassau."

Before any of them could speak up, Lars continued. "This has always been the home of Nassau, an aristocratic family and related to the monarchy. As you know, the late Earl was the Minister of Defense, and his son is now the private secretary to the Prime Minister." Lars finally sat next to Johannes. "Everyone in this house has been here at least a couple of years, except for a few. Tess, Emma, Willem, and Lotte are the new comers......"

Dekker could see a look of discomfort on Lars' face. "Lars, what is it that is making you uncomfortable?" Dekker asked. Lars took a breath and let out a sigh. "Something does not feel right. Something is out of place in House Nassau. In the thirty years of my being here, this is the first time something did not feel right." Johannes spoke up, "What is it that makes you feel this way?" Lars shook his head and did a slight shrug of the shoulders. "I just wanted to tell you, gentlemen, that I cannot shake these feelings."

The clock on the mantle showed eleven twenty. Lars pulled out his pocket watch and grunted slightly. He stood and walked over to correct the time to eleven twenty-five. "Gentlemen, I will now take you to the Earl's study. Please join me now."

As they arrived in the grand hallway outside the Earl's study, the Prime Minister was standing next to the

Minister of Defense. "Gentleman," Bram announced, stepping out of the large study. "The Earl and Countess are ready to meet with you." Everyone entered the large study one by one, led by the Prime Minister. Robert was sitting at a table next to Mary. They had arranged to have tea, coffee, and a small buffet for this morning's meeting. Robert stood and gestured to everyone to find a seat at the table with them. "Please help yourself to something to eat and drink, gentlemen."

Each one bowed to the Earl and Countess Nassau as they arrived at the table. The Prime Minister sighed to himself as he saw his friend appeared to be a different person. "He looks like a man who could kill, he thought to himself. Mary looked like she had not slept in days but was still perfectly dressed. The Prime Minister spoke, "My lord, I want to thank you for taking this time to meet with everyone. I hope you have seen the Royal Police and Royal Marechaussee have been working hard to resolve this for you and your family." Robert did not reply, but Mary spoke up, "We have noticed the dedication of their men to protect Meneer Michael."

Emma and Tess were sitting at the writing desk near to Robert's desk. Emma was shuffling some papers and talking quietly to Tess. Tess had a small portable writing table next to her with Mary's diary and letters on it. Johannes looked to them and asked Robert, "I hope you do not find this to be impertinent, my lord, but may we meet without the secretaries being present?" Robert shook his head, "Emma is working on several documents for the Prime Minister and

I.. Tess is working on several appointments for the countess. We can speak freely around them." Johannes nodded briefly in understanding while taking out his notebook.

After reviewing the events with Robert and Mary, he could confirm the timeline. "We do not know if the attempted kidnapping of Meneer Michael is related to your position as secretary to the Prime Minister, the cousin to Queen Wilhelmina, or just coincidental. Is there anything new in the government that could be related to this incident?" Robert looked over to the Prime Minister. Johannes noticed the glance shared, so did Dekker and Jansen. The two said nothing.

The Prime Minister shifted in his seat slightly. "We have been learning of a new political movement in Germany," said the Prime Minister. Robert looked to Johannes. "My father left me some handwritten letters with his will informing me of what intelligence he could get. The Prime Minister, the new Minister of Defense, and I have been receiving more information about this political movement and their leader."

As Robert continued, he shook his head, "I cannot see how this would be related to the situation with my son." The Prime Minister turned to Robert. "The National Socialist German's Workers Party has sent their members into other countries to get sensitive information." The Prime Minister turned to face the policemen. "We are fearful the leader of this group, an Adolf Hitler, will make himself the leader of the German government. We are getting intelligence that they have people in other governments providing sensitive information to this new political movement."

Johannes started to talk, but was visibly changing his question in his mind. "I understand, my lord, that you work for Her Majesty's government, mainly from here. Are all communications secured?" The Minister of Defense answered for Robert, "All mail, documents, and telephone calls are secured. Documents are handed directly to the Earl, me, or the Prime Minister. "I do not want to step out of place, my lord, but I must know as much as I am allowed. With your recent inheritance to the title, palace, and staff, is there anything that you can think of that would seem out of place?" Johannes asked with a look on his face, requesting sympathy for asking this question. Robert and Mary were simply shaking their heads. Johannes became physically relaxed now that the question was not taken as being impertinent.

Dekker slid over a piece of paper to Johannes. On it was a question that he wanted answered. Johannes took a deep breath and looked at Dekker. He slid it over to Dekker and nodded to him to be the one to ask. "As the Royal Marechaussee representative, I must ask this question. Have you found anything out of place, moved, missing, or signs of theft? Also, my lord, I have to ask how you secure the sensitive documents."

Robert stood and walked over to the bookcase next to the fireplace. Dekker, Jansen, and Johannes sat up slightly more when they saw the very large vault. Each of them could see the dark green vault with the three combination dials on it. Robert closed it and returned to his seat. "Understood," said Dekker. "Who has the combinations to the vault, my lord?"

Robert replied quickly, "Myself, the Prime Minister, and Queen Wilhelmina are the only ones who have the combinations. They were not in my father's documents."

Johannes and Dekker wrote some notes. Before anyone could ask anything more, a knock at the doors ended the awkward silence. Emma stood from her desk and pulled one door ajar. A few moments later, she closed it and walked to Robert. Emma bent over to whisper into Robert's ear. Robert directed Emma, "Please tell Brigadier de Groot," Emma softly spoke, "Sirs, the head groundskeeper is in the entry hall. He is claiming that they found the missing footman in a barn on the estate." Emma's face became pale, and it looked as if she was about to faint. "Alive?" asked Johannes. Emma simply shook her head and walked back to her desk, slightly stumbling from the shock.

Chapter

11

Brigadier Johannes de Groot stood from his chair. "My lord, would you be willing to join us in the barn?" Robert stood and nodded. Mary remained in the study as Robert went to the entry hall with the men.

As they left the study, they found the head groundskeeper standing next to three uniformed Royal Policemen. Everyone in the hall bowed to Robert as the groundskeeper spoke. "My lord, I have found the missing footman's body in the barn at the edge of your estate."

Robert turned to Bram. "Can you please join us to identify the body?" Bram nodded, and everyone walked out the grand front entry. Several vehicles were parked outside to drive them to the barn in question.

The estate was vast and made most of its income from farming. The morning summer air was cool with a slight breeze. The landscape was lush and green this time of year. As they drove towards the barn, crops of wheat and barley could be seen to the south, while the fields of other crops to the north. The rising sun was bright and glorious, but somehow seemed out of place for such a somber turn of events.

They arrived at the massive wooden and stone barn with clay tiled roof. It was simple yet practical for wheat storage and harvesting equipment. Jan, the head groundskeeper, led the men into the barn. "My men came into the barn this morning to get some equipment and saw the large canvas laundry basket," pointing to the far corner. "It is clearly out of place here, so my men looked in and found Antoon." The Brigadier, Dekker, and Jansen walked up to the large canvas laundry bag and looked down.

The canvas bag was three meters in diameter and three meters in depth, large enough to conceal a full-sized man's body. Inside was the body of a man in a footman's uniform. Bram slowly walked up to the bag but then quickly ran out of the barn to be sick outside. Dekker directed everyone out of the barn.

When they got outside, he handed Bram a handkerchief. "My lord, this confirms a suspicion Brigadier de Groot had. Your missing footman was the victim of a murder, and the blood in the laundry was his." Robert turned away from the barn to prevent breathing in the continued smell. "I will return to my study and would appreciate regular updates from this point on." Robert got into the vehicle, taking the Prime Minister, the Minister of Defense, and Bram with him.

Inspector Jansen and Brigadier de Groot remained inside the barn to assess the scene. Several more Rijkspolitie and Royal Marechaussee men arrived. Dekker walked over to Jan and requested he call for the royal physician from the palace to come down. Jan nodded and stepped out of the barn. Jansen looked around to see a remnant of last season's wheat harvest on the ground, tools hanging from the walls and beams, as well as other farm equipment scattered. The laundry bag looked to have been dumped with some haste in the corner. "Must have expected this would go unfound for several months due to fall harvesting," Jansen stated without expecting a response.

Dekker and the Brigadier were inspecting the body of Antoon. "Looks to have been stabbed in the back and once in the chest," Dekker stated. Johannes was carefully looking at the man's uniform. "Most stab wounds are in his back."

As Johannes finished his statement, Doctor Arends walked into the barn. "What have you found, gentlemen?" the doctor asked as he approached. Dekker and Johannes backed away from the laundry bag. "Dear God!" exclaimed Doctor Arends, "Poor man!" Dekker, de Groot, Jansen, and the doctor pulled Antoon's body from the canvas laundry bag.

As they placed him on his back, the men could see a stab wound to his chest. "Help me roll him onto his side," stated Doctor Arends. Dekker rolled Antoon onto his right side, and the doctor counted four additional wounds to his back. "They were determined to kill this poor man," said Arends. Antoon's head and face were a purple color, and his tongue swollen and dark. A rope was still around Antoon's ankles and wrists. Johannes stood and yelled out, "Bastards!" Before the others could ask anything, Johannes continued. "They hung the poor man from his ankles and tortured him, but why?" The Inspector walked over to his friend. "Why would they torture a footman?" Johannes looked at Jan and shook his head.

Doctor Arends turned to Johannes. "Do we have family information for him?"

Johannes pulled out his notebook and read out what information he had for Antoon. "The butler could get a home address for Antoon's mother in Gouda," Johannes said as he copied the information down for the doctor.

The Royal Police carried the body of Antoon out of the barn. Doctor Arends followed and told Johannes that he would have his office contact the mother for official identification. "I will go with them," said Dekker. Jansen and de Groot agreed to that arrangement. "I will return tomorrow; my family is in Gouda, and I will stay there this evening. Shall I bring either of you anything?"

"Stroopwafels," requested Johannes. Dekker nodded and walked out.

A small stool was hanging on the wall, and Jansen took it down and sat next to the laundry bag. "How difficult would it have been to bring Antoon in this all the way to the barn?" asked Jansen. Johannes lifted the bag with one of the handles. "How much would you say Antoon weighed?" asked Johannes. "He was about my build."

"I would say close to ninety kilograms." Jansen said. Johannes nodded and replied, "I cannot see a single man moving a dead body in this. Let alone all the way from the laundry to here." The two lifted the large canvas laundry bag to look at the bottom. "What do we have here?!" exclaimed Jansen. With a gloved hand, he pulled up a red wig to show Johannes. "Look what I have found under our laundry bag."

Johannes expression was of anger and confusion. "Why? What? Who?" stuttered Johannes, taking the wig from his friend. As he turned away, Inspector Jansen was confused with Johannes' response. Jansen was used to Johannes being the one never frustrated, or at least never expressing it.

Inspector Jansen directed the Royal Policemen still in the barn to complete an inventory and search of the barn inside and outside. As he walked out of the barn with Johannes, he turned back, "We should make another search of all outbuildings." The Royal Policemen all saluted the Inspector and began their assignments.

The two entered the palace at the main entrance to be greeted by Lars in the main hallway. "Sirs, is it true?" Lars was hoping it was Bram's imagination. "I am afraid that it was Antoon, and he was stabbed several times," responded Jansen. "Lars, do you know how many of the large canvas laundry bags the palace has?" Lars shook his head no. "You will need to speak with

Fleur about that" Lars apologized. "How is Bram doing now?" asked Johannes. Lars was visually concerned as well. "I sent him to his rooms. I understand he became sick at the sight of his friend's body." Jansen and Johannes nodded and said they would like to check on Bram.

Lars handed the two a key from his keyring. "This will get you entry to the staff entrance to the male side. Please let me know if Bram requires anything." Johannes led the way up the servants' stairs to the staff level. After using the key to gain access, they walked down to the first footman's door.

Upon knocking, the door became ajar. Jansen knocked again, and the door continued to open. They could see Bram sitting on a chair in his sitting room. Bram turned his head to them. "Please come in, gentlemen."

Inspector Jansen and the Brigadier walked in and sat by Bram. "Are you alright sir?" asked Johannes. "I…I do not know," replied Bram. A knock on the door frame revealed the fifth footman arriving with a tray. "Lars asked me to bring this up." Bram gestured the young footman into his rooms. After putting the tray on a table, Bram thanked him, and he walked out, closing the door. "Lars is very formal and based on protocol, gentlemen. But he is kind to us, as you can see by this tray." Lars sent up tea, coffee, cakes, breads, and some other basic snacks.

Under one cup was a note with Bram's name written on it. "My dear man, please take the rest of the day off and stay in bed. I can manage with the other staff."

"I cannot imagine having to see a friend's dead body, especially in that manner," stated Johannes. Bram, still sitting back in the chair, said, "I cannot express what I feel, gentlemen." Johannes nodded. "Are you feeling up to a couple of questions?" Bram nodded, "Go ahead." Johannes pulled the red wig out of his suit jacket. "Do you recognize this, sir?" Bram looked but shook his head no. "Do you know how many of the canvas laundry bags the palace has?" Johannes put the wig back into his pocket. Bram thought for a moment. "We have four of the size you found Antoon in. We have several small ones that we keep around the palace. We use the large ones to sort the laundry. There is a pulley system on the ceiling in the laundry to lift the larger ones." The Brigadier and the Inspector thanked Bram for his time and gave their condolences.

As the two walked down the staff stairs, Johannes spoke, "I cannot imagine having to identify my best friend's body." The Inspector did not respond, he just shook his head no in agreement. Once in the basement, they walked directly to the laundry. A uniformed Royal Policeman was still being posted at the door. He handed Johannes the key and stepped to the side. Johannes put the key into the lock, but did not turn it. "How could anyone get to the barn from here?" Johannes thought out loud.

After unlocking the door and stepping in, the Brigadier looked up to find the pulley system. A loud sigh came from the Brigadier. "They hung Antoon from this pulley and allowed him to bleed out before moving his body. The laundry bag was purely to hide the body in the barn." Johannes looked over to the Inspector, "Open the door to the back garden, please."

The two walked around the short corner and opened the door. They looked at the ground and saw that the grass was undisturbed but looked to have been cut recently. "I wonder if the gardener cut the grass before or after Michael was taken?" asked the Inspector. He continued back in and asked the policeman stationed there to get that question answered.

The head cook stood at the end of the hallway and beckoned to the two. Johannes signaled she could come to them as he closed the door to the laundry. Cornelia walked up and asked the two, "When can we use the laundry again? We have several table linens, bed linens, and uniforms that need washing." Johannes apologized and asked, "Can they be washed at one of the estate cottages?" Cornelia had an expression that showed she did not like that question. "We have a large amount of linen; the cottage washrooms could not handle the amount easily." Johannes relented and said, "You may use the laundry, unfortunately, it will not be a pleasant task to clean it first. Johannes remembered her response to blood.

"There is a fair amount of blood left on the floor, Mevrouw Cornelia. May I suggest that you do not enter until it has been cleaned?"

Cornelia left to tell her sister that they could open the laundry once again, but the task would not be an easy one. As Cornelia turned out of their sight, Jansen said, "I do not wish that chore to my worst enemy" and walked down to their temporary quarters.

As they arrived at their door, they found a message pinned to the door. The note said, "Major Dekker telephoned that Antoon's mother was home and not strong enough to identify Antoon's body tonight. The Major will take her tomorrow morning before he returns to Palace Nassau." They walked into the bedroom and locked the wig into the safe with the other evidence. "Do you want to meet with Willem or should I?" asked Johannes. Inspector Jansen agreed to meet with Willem and asked Johannes, "Anything specific you want me to ask?" Johannes shook his head no, "Just ask what you feel is necessary." Johannes remained in their sitting room while Jansen went to Meneer Michael's room.

At the top of the stairs, one of his men met him. "Hallo, Inspector, how is the investigation going?" The Inspector shook his head and replied, "Slowly, and I think the Brigadier has figured out several things about it." He was now walking to Michael's room.

After knocking on Willem's bedroom door, Willem answered quickly. "Hallo Inspector, please come in. Michael is awake, and Charles is in the library with his parents. The Duke and Duchess had recently arrived." Willem walked the Inspector into Meneer Michael's room to find him sitting in a chair by the windows.

"Hallo, Meneer Michael. My name is Inspector Jansen with the Rijkspolitie." Michael did not even look at him, only out the windows. "I promised your father that we would find the man that did that to you, and I want you to know we found Antoon." Michael turned around to look at Jansen. "I am sorry to say that he is dead," said Jansen. Michael looked down at the floor, then stood. He said one word after he stood, "Father." Willem walked over to him and asked, "You want me to take you to the Earl?" Michael nodded and pointed to the hidden passage door.

Inspector Jansen led the way, followed by Michael and Willem. "My Lord!" announced Inspector Jansen as he opened the passage in the large study. Robert was alone when he saw his son. Robert ran to Michael and picked him up and squeezed him tightly. "Antoon is dead, father." Robert put his son down and said, "I know, my dear boy." They walked over to the sofa by the fireplace. "How are you feeling, Michael?" asked Robert. Michael replied, "Scared!" Robert asked Willem to find the others and bring them to his study.

Only a few minutes later, Willem returned with Mary, Charles, the Duke and Duchess of Luxly, and Lars. Mary and Charles ran over to Michael and wrapped their arms around Michael. "Meneer Michael, would you like something to eat?" asked Lars. Michael simply replied, "I am hungry, thank you." Lars immediately left and, once out of sight, ran to the kitchens. The Duke and Duchess walked up to Michael.

When the Duke hugged Michael, he whispered, "You are stronger than you think. You are the bloodline to this family and must remain strong." Michael nodded and asked Willem to come over to him. "I heard you talking to someone outside my room last night, but I could not understand." Willem had to explain to

Michael that the palace was full of Royal Police and Royal Marechaussee. "You were Marechaussee?" asked Michael. Willem nodded, "That is why I am going to be with you at all times." Michael looked and noticed that Willem had a handgun under his suit jacket.

As Lars returned with food and drinks for Michael, he set up on a small table. Two footmen also entered with additional food and drinks for the others. "Meneer Michael, are you feeling up to answering some questions while you eat?" Michael looked to his father, and Robert said, "Only if you feel up to it."

Inspector Jansen sat opposite Michael. Lars handed Jansen a cup of coffee before he asked Michael his questions. Lars whispered to Jansen, "Gently," while giving a look of protection on his face. Jansen adjusted himself in the seat. "I only want you to tell me what you remember about who took you." Michael finished chewing his food and swallowed loudly. Michael closed his eyes. "He was tall because my feet did not touch the floor. I did not know his voice or his accent. He told me he would kill me if I screamed. I still tried, but his hand covered my mouth. And he smelled like mint tobacco…pipe tobacco." The Inspector asked if anyone at the estate smoked a pipe, but the consensus was only cigars and cigarettes. The Inspector stood up and asked for someone to get Brigadier de Groot from their temporary quarters.

As he waited, the Minister of Defense walked into the room. Jansen motioned to join him on the opposite side of the room. "Sir, it is our opinion that Antoon was attempting to contact the Royal Marechaussee for some reason. We do not want to announce this to anyone, but I feel you, being the Minister of Defense, should know now that we have found his body."

The Minister moved so his back was turned to the others. "Have you found Antoon to be a member of Her Majesty's government?" The Inspector shook his head no.

Brigadier de Groot knocked and entered the study and bowed. "Meneer Michael, I am thrilled to see you are recovering," Johannes said as he looked at Michael. Michael walked over to de Groot and looked at him up and down. The Brigadier looked like a soldier to Michael, just in a suit. Michael reached out and shook Johannes' hand. "I have told the Inspector what I remember from when I was taken. do you have questions?" Johannes smiled, "Not at this time, my lord." Michael took Johannes' right hand and looked at the signet ring.

As he looked up to Johannes and asked, "You are a knight, sir?" Johannes cleared his throat, "I am, Meneer Michael." Everyone in the room now had their attention directed to de Groot. He continued, "Your cousin awarded me my title Knight Grand Cross in 1918 after the war ended." Michael smiled, "Why do you not use your formal title, sir?" Johannes smiled and bent over slightly and whispered to Michael, "The criminals are more afraid of Brigadier de Groot." Johannes returned to his upright, almost at attention position.

After he bowed to Michael, the young man saluted

him. "I may wish to speak with you later, Meneer Michael, with your father's permission." Robert looked to Johannes, "My son may make his own decisions, Brigadier. He does not need my permission to speak with the police."

Chapter

12

The following morning, Johannes had an experiment that he wanted to test. The Brigadier walked through the halls and selected ten uniformed officers to conduct the experiment. Five were with the Rijkspolitie, and the other five were Marechaussee.

Each of the men were of different heights and builds. Jan and Dekker stood outside with the large laundry bag that Antoon was found in, with several bags of flower and sugar. After lining up each officer based on height, Johannes explained the experiment to everyone. "I have instructed my colleagues to load this laundry bag with the same amount of weight that the killed footman was. Antoon weighed exactly 80 kg according to Dr. Arends. As you can see, I want each of you to attempt to take this laundry bag with 80 kg from this door all the way to the barn where Antoon was found. Only one of you can do this at a time."

Johannes walked over to the smallest officer first. "I want you to take the challenge first, young man." The smallest officer grabbed both handles and walked while pulling. As Daan, Jan, and Johannes watched, they could see this would not be an easy or quick task.

They timed each attempt. The first attempt made it 30 meters.

One by one, each officer attempted to take the laundry bag to the barn. Each officer made it a little further than the previous one. Only the last two officers could get the laundry bag with 80 kg of weight to the barn. The last two could complete the test within fifteen minutes.

Johannes sat down on a stool inside the barn while the others cleaned up. In his notes, he jotted down the information learned from his experiment. Dekker walked over, "I think we know that this was not a small man." Johannes nodded in agreement. Just then, Lars walked into the barn. "I could not see from the cottages, sir." Johannes turned and thanked Lars.

House Nassau has four estate cottages. They were built in the early 1800s or senior staff. The cottages are on the other side of the lake. Tess resides in the first cottage, and the twins were in the second. Emma resides in the third, with Lars in the last one. Each cottage was identical in floor plan and furniture. Staff can decorate with some personal items like photos. Lars had provided the master keys to Johannes the night before. The Brigadier and the Inspector would conduct the searches at the cottages without Dekker. Major Dekker would travel to Breda today.

As Johannes and the Inspector walked down the trail to the cottages, two uniformed Rijkspolitie met them. "Gentlemen, please join us to the cottages." Johannes directed them to follow. As they arrived, they could see that all the cottages faced Palace Nassau over the small lake. Parts of the garden and the servants' door in question are not visible from the cottages.

Johannes took out the master keys from his pocket and unlocked the cottage assigned to Tess. As they walked in, they saw the stairs leading to the first floor. The ground floor contained a sitting room with a fireplace and several small pieces of furniture. Several pictures of what appeared to be family were neatly arranged on a side table. A small kitchen and scullery are in the back. Connected to the scullery was a small laundry. "Tess is very tidy, I see," said Jansen.

Johannes walked up the narrow and steep staircase to the first floor. There were two small bedrooms with a bathroom and a toilet. The first bedroom was obviously a guest room, and there were no personal items visible. The second bedroom was filled with perfumes, pictures, and some plants.

"Rather crowded in here," announced Johannes. The Brigadier called down for one of the policemen to come up. "Please take full inventory of these rooms."

The policeman began his assignment directly. As Johannes walked back down, he saw Jansen going through the small desk by the door leading to the kitchen. "Are you finding anything of interest?" he asked. "Not as of yet, but look at these," as he handed

Johannes several letters. "These appear to be letters from a love interest." Johannes sat down on the sofa as he looked through them. "I wonder who the man is?" replied Jansen. The Inspector already tasked the other policeman with taking the ground floors inventory. Johannes handed the letters back to Jansen and walked over to some photos.

As he picked one up, he could hear the policeman upstairs call out his name. "What is it?" he replied. "I have found a key, sir, but nothing up here takes a key." Johannes walked up and took the key. Where did you find this?" asked the Brigadier. The policeman held up an antique box. "This was in her chest of drawers." Johannes gave a quick nod and went back down. "Jan, do you see what this would unlock?" The Inspector turned to look at the key. "It looks like it goes to this desk," pointing to the drawer.

Johannes walked over and handed the key to the Inspector. As he turned it, he stated, "It works." Inspector Jansen pulled the desk drawer open to find papers from a bank and some gilders. Nothing else was in the drawer, so he relocked it. Johannes was still holding the photo. It was a picture of Tess with an older couple standing in front of Dam Palace in Amsterdam. "Looks to be Tess with her parents," announced Johannes.

The two uniformed policemen completed the inventory of the first cottage. The four stepped out, and Johannes locked the door. As they walked over to the second cottage, the Inspector asked, "Will we be interviewing everyone tonight?" Johannes nodded and unlocked the door.

The four stepped into find an identical situation. Johannes looked around and commented, "The twins have a lot of belongings." The Inspector sat at the desk, but it was in a different spot than Tess'. The twins placed their desk in the kitchen. "I do not think that we will find anything in here, at least I hope not, for Dekker's sake.

"I will start in the bedrooms," announced the Brigadier as he walked up the steep staircase. The first bedroom looked to be occupied by Fleur, as it contained several pictures of her with a man dressed in a military uniform. The bedroom was neatly organized as you would expect from a professional housekeeper. Cornelia's was the opposite. The bed was not made, items of clothing were thrown over a chair, and some dirty uniforms were on the floor.

Johannes went back down to find Jan in the laundry. "Do you think the sisters could move a body?" The Inspector continued, "They are both use to physical labor after all." The Brigadier lifted the smaller canvas laundry bag. "I have no doubt that they are stronger than most women, but I do not think they could drag him all the way to the barn."

The two policemen came into the laundry to announce they completed with their inventory. As the four walked out, Lars was standing outside Emma's door. "I wanted to let you gentlemen know I heard Emma and Tess announce they would take their midday meals in their cottages." A loud grunt came from

Johannes. "Are you able to distract them from coming to the cottages?" Lars looked displeased at being given the task. "I guess I could attempt an excuse, sir." The four policemen stepped into Emma's cottage.

Emma's cottage was arranged completely different from the others. "It appears to be missing some furniture," said one of the policemen. Johannes went up to find that the second bedroom did not have any furniture.

While the policemen took inventory of Emma's bedroom, the Brigadier returned to the ground floor. The sitting room was missing several pieces of furniture that the other two had. Emma's cottage did not have a desk either. Several personal papers were found in an old hatbox in the sitting room.

While the Inspector looked through them, Johannes went into the laundry. "What did Bram say about the laundry being done in the cottages?" Jan spoke up, "That each one does their own." Jansen leaned out, "Then why does it appear that Emma does not do laundry here?" The Inspector stood and joined the Brigadier in the laundry. "How does she not do laundry?" asked Jan.

The policemen came down from the first floor. "Brigadier, Emma does not have much to search through." Johannes took the notepad from the man. "She does not have much here at all," as he reads through the notes.

They were satisfied that they had looked through

everything. As they stepped out, they were met by Lars again. "I told them that the cottages were being worked on, and that the water is not working at this time." Both Jan and Johannes smiled. "You are a clever man, Lars," said Johannes. "Thank you, sir," he replied. "Do you know why Emma's cottage is missing furniture, or why she does not use the laundry?' Lars nodded. Emma does her laundry with Tess in the first cottage. And for the lack of furniture, it is still in the attics.

Emma came to us late, and we have yet to finish setting it up for her. The situation with Antoon and Meneer Michael has delayed it." Both Jan and Johannes nodded in understanding. "We just have your cottage left, Lars. We will schedule a time that we can meet everyone in their cottage after.

Lars' cottage was the cleanest and most organized of all the cottages. Each item had a place, and each item was well organized. "There is nothing out of place in there," said Jan.

Johannes sat in the armchair next to the fireplace. He could see photos of Lars' family were arranged next to the wireless. Jan sat at the desk placed next to the kitchen door. "I wish my desk was this tidy," said Jan, then he laughed.

As Johannes walked into the kitchen, he could see that the butler took order to a whole new level. "I think our butler could teach at the training center." Jan replied, "He would scare the recruits away."

On the first floor, they found the bathroom and bedrooms in the same organized fashion. Johannes laughed, "It does not look like anyone even lives in here." The policeman handed Johannes his notes. "I could complete this easier than the others, sir, the butler even organizes his underclothing."

The four sat in Lars' sitting room. After the Brigadier told the Inspector his plans, they walked back to the palace. As they were walking, the Inspector puts his hand on his friend's shoulder. "I hope that the stress of this case is not overwhelming you, my friend." Johannes shrugged. "I may retire after this is solved." Johannes had a depressed look on his face now. As they walked into the old cook's rooms, the clock chimed one o'clock. Johannes sat down and started writing his instructions for Lars. "After the family has their evening meal, we will interview Tess. I think an hour in each cottage should be enough." Johannes finished the note and called out to one of the Rijkspolitie in the hallway. "Please take this to the butler; he will know what it is about."

Johannes and Jan ate their evening meal in the old cook's rooms. The two decided to eat their meals early to allow for the extra time before their interviews. Lars arrived with a tray containing tea and desserts. "Would you like to start with me, gentlemen?" Johannes answered as he took some cake. "We would like to start with Tess. We will conduct the interviews in the cottages as well." Lars gave a small nod as Johannes returned the master keys.

The mantel clock chimed six thirty as Johannes closed

and locked the door to the old cook's rooms. Johannes and Jan started their walk to the cottages. They saw Emma walking ahead of them, as well as Fleur and Cornelia. They were followed by two uniformed Rijkspolitie.

Johannes knocked on Tess's cottage door. It took but a few moments for Tess to answer. As she opened the door, the men noticed the amazing smell of freshly baked bread wafted through the air. Tess gestured for them to sit. "Please, gentlemen, make yourselves comfortable. I have fresh tea, and I have bread and fresh jam." Jan and Johannes thanked her and helped themselves. The Inspector spoke first. "I am Inspector Jan Jansen with the Rijkspolitie. My colleague is Brigadier Johannes de Groot. He will ask all the questions tonight. I will take notes for him." Tess nodded in understanding as she sat on the sofa opposite them.

Chapter

13

Johannes took a drink before beginning his questions, but an odd expression crossed his face as he sipped.

"Is there a problem, Brigadier?" Tess asked.

"This is the best tea I have ever tasted," Johannes exclaimed. "Thank you, sir. The tea comes from my travels to China last year."

"I understand you were assigned to Countess Nassau and went to London. Do you know how you were chosen for this position?" Tess nodded. "I applied for it when I was told it was available. My sister works for Noordeinde Palace."

"What was your job before working here?" Tess smiled. "I'm sure you already know that answer, sir."

"Please, just answer the question, even if you think I know."

"I worked at Dam Palace as a secretary for several government officials. There were six of us in the same office."

"What interested you in working for the Nassau's?" Tess poured more tea and took a moment to choose her words carefully. "To work for one of the great families of our country—who wouldn't want that opportunity?"

"Can you walk me through a typical day for you?" She leaned back on the sofa. "I wake at seven every morning, I am expected in Her Ladyship's study at eight. She still works with several charities in London and, now, here in the Netherlands. I open and screen letters daily, type correspondence, and help arrange events for the family. My day usually ends by the evening meal."

"Do you remember where you were when Meneer Michael was taken?" Tess's face grew pale and somber. "I was in the Earl's study with Emma. We were both working on letters for the Earl and Countess."

"Do you recall where the Earl and Countess were at that time?" Tess nodded and took a large bite of bread with jam. After swallowing, she answered. "They were in the Royal Delft Blue Room with the butler. They were selecting pieces from their collection, preparing for the Queen's visit."

"Do you know much about Antoon?" She shook her head. "I know he worked here for some time, but I do not interact much with the house staff." Johannes noticed a look of displeasure on her face that prompted his next question. "Why don't you interact with the house staff?" Tess looked down. "They don't consider us house staff, so they do not include us. Lars, Fleur, and Cornelia barely look at us, even here at the cottages.

"When was the last time you saw Antoon?" She thought for a moment. "I believe I saw him walking with Meneer Michael and the young Marquess going up the main stairs the night before Michael went missing."

"Have you seen or heard anything out of the ordinary?" Tess shook her head. "You work directly for the Earl and Countess. Surely you must overhear private conversations. I will not ask you to break their trust, but have you heard anything concerning?" Again, Tess shook her head.

"With your role, do you always work closely with Emma?" Tess nodded. "Do the two of you only talk about work, or do you discuss other matters?" She smiled. "Are you asking if Emma and I have become friends, sir?" Johannes chuckled. "In a way. Do you talk about your private lives?" Tess nodded again. "We have become friends. Our jobs can be lonely, and we keep each other company at work and on our days off."

"What can you tell me about Emma?" Tess flushed. "I will not speak about her when she's not here."

"I'll ask her the same questions about you," the Brigadier said gently.

Tess's body language stiffened, showing her frustration. "She grew up in Breda with an older brother. Her father died when she was about ten years of age; her mother died of influenza a few years later.

Her brother raised her from the age of thirteen. I think he served in the Great War but was injured… she never said how."

"Do you or Emma have men in your lives?" Tess nearly choked on her tea. "No, sir," she said, blushing. "Thank you for your time, Tess. We'll take our leave now. The tea, bread, and jam were excellent."

Johannes and Jan let themselves out of Tess's cottage and made their way to the cottage occupied by Fleur and Cornelia. As they approached, they saw Fleur waiting outside. "Goedeavond," Fleur greeted the two policemen as they arrived. She had let her hair down from its work bun; it now fell to her waist. Her pale face lit up with a smile. "Gentlemen, please come in. My sister and I are ready to answer your questions."

Fleur led them inside. Cornelia and Fleur were definitely identical twins, and with their hair down, the resemblance was even clearer. Cornelia sat in an armchair by the fireplace. As she sitting her teacup down, she rose to greet the policemen.

The two policemen sat together on the sofa, facing the small fireplace so they could see both sisters.

Jan spoke first. "The Brigadier will ask all the questions. I'm here to take notes. Please direct your answers to him." The sisters nodded in understanding. Cornelia handed the Brigadier and the Inspector cups of tea. "I would like to know where you both were when Meneer Michael was taken," Fleur answered first. "We were in the kitchen planning the evening meals. The Countess still takes afternoon tea and prefers it before the midday meal. We were loading the tray when we were told…" Cornelia set down her cup, looking sad. She seemed about to speak but stopped herself.

"Go ahead, Cornelia," Fleur encouraged. "I just find this so hard to understand, gentlemen. Meneer Michael and the young Marquess were in the kitchens not long before… Antoon was very popular here. I do not see how these situations are connected — but also do not see how they could not be."

Johannes nodded sympathetically. "I agree. It is difficult, but I believe Antoon's death and the attempted kidnapping are connected." The Inspector took a sip of tea and grimaced slightly — it was not as good as he would have hoped, though the sisters did not notice. Johannes opened his notebook to a page marked with an X. "Can you tell me anything about Tess or Emma?" The question visibly unsettled both Fleur and Cornelia.

"They are private staff to the Earl and Countess. There is nothing else to tell," Fleur said. "So, neither one of you knows anything about them?" Fleur replied, "They sometimes eat with the family when there are no guests. Otherwise, they prepare their own meals." Johannes continued to press gently for more information. "Do you like Tess or Emma?" The sisters shrugged in unison. "We barely know them," Cornelia added. "Both are new to the palace."

"Antoon was popular. Why?" Cornelia answered first. "He was always willing to help. He would even pitch in with cleaning up the kitchen." Fleur nodded. "He would ask if I needed anything, too."

"Was that unusual for a footman?" Johannes asked. Both sisters nodded. "They have their own tasks, but he was never too busy to help," Fleur said.

"Have you noticed anything odd or different around the palace?" Fleur glanced out the window. "The new staff caused some strife when they arrived. The cottages were not ready. Lars, Bram, and Antoon were busy preparing for the family." Johannes showed a look of confusion. Cornelia explained, "Lars had the footmen bringing furniture down from the attic. They were delayed because of the arriving guests."

"You mentioned that this caused a problem. Please explain." Fleur cleared her throat. "Emma's cottage was not ready when she arrived. She was angry, and she reminded everyone she was the Earl's secretary." Cornelia added, "Lars tried to explain the delay, but she would not accept it."

"Now that Meneer Michael has started to recover, has he returned to the kitchens or passages?" Both sisters shook their heads. "But it is always a pleasure to see him and the Marquess. We even showed them the passage doors on the maps they drew," they said.

"Is it possible to move from the staff areas to the outdoors without being seen or heard?" The sisters thought for a moment. "There are no passages to the outdoors, sir. And none of the doors are hidden from staff areas. There's always someone below stairs who would see anyone out of place."

Fleur turned to Cornelia. "Would the hall boy or scullery maid hear anything at night?" Cornelia nodded. "You may want to speak to them. They are the only staff awake during the night."

Johannes drank the last of his tea and wrote down: hall boy and scullery maid.

"When did you last see Antoon?"

"The night before, in the staff dining room. We went back to our cottage before the house staff went to their rooms."

"Thank you, ladies. We will take our leave now. One last question — do you know if Antoon had anyone special in his life?" Both sisters shook their heads. "He never mentioned anyone to us," Fleur said.

Before heading to Emma's cottage, Johannes lit a cigarette. Jan noticed the familiar look on his friend's face. Just as Jan was about to speak, Johannes started to rub his beard. A slight smile crossed Jan's face. "I know when you rub that thing, you are thinking or have reached a conclusion. Which is it?" Johannes did not reply — he just smiled at his friend. After flicking away the cigarette, Johannes knocked on Emma's door. She answered, and greeting them warmly. "Goedeavond, heren. Please, come in and have a seat." Johannes and Jan entered the sitting room. "Ah!" Johannes exclaimed. "I see that Bram has brought more of the furniture down for you." The missing furniture was indeed now in place, including the small writing desk the other cottages had. "He brought them down an hour ago. I assume you have searched the cottages already." Emma said.

Neither Johannes nor Jan replied. They simply sat together on the sofa. Emma had prepared tea and set out Stroopwafels. "These are my guilty pleasure," Johannes said, placing one atop his teacup to warm. Emma looked timid in her green summer dress, her hair braided. The round black glasses made her face seem rounder still. Johannes thought to himself, "Very unfortunate woman."

Jan began his introduction, but Emma stopped him. "Gentlemen, I understand you have a difficult task, but I will not answer questions about the Earl's role or our conversations without him being present." Johannes and Jan exchanged a glance as Jan explained he would only be taking notes.

Emma was not as timid as she appeared. "Can you confirm where you were and what you were doing when Meneer Michael was taken?"

"I was with Tess in the Earl's study. We both had work to complete for the Earl and Countess."

"Where were the Earl and Countess at that time?"

"They were in the Royal Delft Room with the butler, going over the collection before the royal visit. The Earl and Countess wanted to choose some pieces for the occasion."

"I understand you spoke with Antoon the night before he disappeared. What did you talk about?" Emma's body language shifted; she was clearly uncomfortable. "I spoke to him in the kitchen as I was leaving for the evening. He asked me how I was settling in and said he would come to my cottage to finish setting up the furniture the next day."

"How did you respond?" After refilling her tea, she replied thoughtfully. "I said I was adjusting slowly, moving from my previous job to life in a palace. He said he had been here a few years and enjoyed it. I asked him to come before the family's evening meal if he could. I was eager to get the cottage finished to help me settle in."

"You worked in Breda before, is that correct? Are you from there originally?"

She nodded and set down her teacup. "Yes, I was born in Breda. After my parents died, my brother raised me in our family home. I worked for Her Majesty's government at the Netherlands Defense Academy as a secretary to several professors."

"What made you change positions?" Emma looked offended. "I was told a position was available as private secretary to the Earl. It meant taking orders from one person instead of several. Plus, I would have my own cottage and would not have to share a home with my brother."

"Does your brother still live in Breda?" She nodded. "What does he do for work?"

"What does my brother have to do with this, sir?" she asked, irritated.

"Please, just answer the question." Emma adjusted in her seat, raising her voice slightly. "He owns a bakery. His name is Alexi Smith, if you need that information." Both the Brigadier and Inspector noted her snide tone.

"I understand you and Tess spend most of your time together. And that the house staff do not consider you part of their ranks — is that correct?" Emma poured more tea and handed the tray of stroopwafels to Johannes. "Yes. Tess and I keep each other company. We work closely, and the house staff do not include us. We have become friends as a result."

The Brigadier leaned back on the couch, stroking his beard before asking, "What is your opinion on what happened here?" Emma looked puzzled. "How do you mean, Brigadier?"

"Exactly that. What do you think happened?" Emma thought for a moment, then looked back to him. "I do not know. None of it makes sense. First, the footman goes missing.

Then someone tries to take Meneer Michael, and Antoon's body was found in a barn. At first, I thought Antoon had tried to take the boy, but then his body was discovered." Johannes studied her quietly. "What is it, sir?" Emma asked, her tone disapproving. "I was waiting to see if you had anything to add." She shook her head no. "Then we will take our leave. Thank you for your time."

Lars was the last interview of the evening. Johannes planned more questions for him, knowing Lars was likely the most observant of the staff — perhaps of any man Johannes had met outside the police.

On their short walk to Lars's cottage, Johannes said, "Some of the questions I have for Lars may shock you, my friend."

Jan did not hesitate. "I trust your methods, Johannes — even when they are not clear to me." When Lars opened the door, Johannes began at once. "I have several questions, sir. Some may not seem relevant, and some may upset you, or be difficult for you to answer." Lars's expression didn't change. "Please, come in, gentlemen," he said, gesturing to the sitting room.

As the Brigadier and the Inspector sat down, Jan noticed a difference in his friend.

Johannes was sitting at the edge of the chair and faced Lars directly. "I must be direct and ask you several questions that will not be easy to answer," said Johannes. Lars sat back on the small sofa and nodded. "Have you found any of the staff fraternizing?" Lars, clearly uncomfortable, nodded his head and replied, "The previous second footman got a housemaid pregnant." Johannes looked to the floor. "Have you found Antoon fraternizing with anyone?" Lars shook his head no.

Johannes pressed on. "I want you to set aside loyalties. Have you seen, heard, or felt anything wrong — before or since the new Earl's family arrived?" Lars leaned forward and poured tea for all three, the best either policeman had tasted.

After ten minutes of silence, Lars set down his cup. "I cannot say anything troubled me before they arrived, but since then... well, there has been something off. I cannot put my finger on it. There were moments that made me uncomfortable. Emma, Tess, and Lotte have asked the staff a lot about the family — questions that felt inappropriate. Emma even asked Bram why the Earl and Countess are so close to Meneer Michael. Somehow, she learned they had several miscarriages before Michael." Johannes and Jan sat back, digesting this. They drank their tea as Johannes jotted notes.

Lars continued. "I overheard Antoon offering to help Emma and Tess on their first day. They told Bram a simple footman could not help with anything beyond dishes or drinks. That is why the house staff have an issue with them."

Johannes stood and walked over to one of the sitting-room windows. As he looked out and absorbed the view of the lake and House Nassau, he could hear some motion from the next cottage. "Can you hear your neighbor all the time through these walls Lars?" asked Johannes. Lars stood up and walked over to the stairs. "I can always hear when Emma is walking around or even talking to someone. I must add that I cannot hear what she is saying because it is always muffled." Lars could tell by the Brigadier's face that he was disappointed in that fact of not being able to understand conversations.

As they were done with their questions, Johannes requested a meeting with the scullery maid and the hall boy. Lars nodded. "They sleep during the daylight hours because they are the only ones awake at night." Lars walked over to his writing desk and wrote two names. Johannes took the note and saw the two names, "Nora Visser and Pieter de Jong." Lars looked to the two policemen and requested, "Please be gentle to both of them. They are both orphans, and that is why they are here. The late Earl took them in and gave them work, food, housing, and a regular pay. They report to work at nine o'clock every night."

After interviewing everyone in the cottages, Johannes and Jan returned to the old cooks quarters. Cornelia knocked on the door, and Johannes opened it to find a young woman next to Cornelia. "This is Nora Visser. She is the scullery maid. Lars has requested I bring her to meet you, gentlemen. Please remember she is only thirteen years old," softly stated Cornelia. Johannes gestured for the two to enter. Jan was sitting in one of the chairs, but quickly stood up to greet them. "Please, ladies, have a seat," as Jan gestured to the two empty chairs. Cornelia sat close to Johannes, and the young Nora sat close to Jan. Nora was clearly visibly shaken about the meeting. "Please have no fear, Nora," said Johannes, "My name is Inspector de Groot, and I am investigating the murder of Antoon and the attempted kidnapping of Meneer Michael."

Cornelia took one of the young girls hands into hers, "Just answer the questions these men ask of you honestly, and we will be done quickly," said Cornelia with an aunt-like tone.

Johannes sat back in the chair and started to pull out his notebook, but changed his mind quickly. "Can you tell me if you have seen anyone on the nights leading up to Meneer Michael's kidnapping walking around?" Nora looked at both Johannes and Jan and quickly replied with, "Only Pieter and I are up at night, sirs." Johannes continued, "So nobody, including family, were walking around at night, especially down here?" The young Nora just shook her head no. Jan handed his friend a piece of paper with a question written on it. Johannes looked at Jan and thought for a moment.

After thinking for a moment, he asked the question. "Do you know how someone could get Antoon's body from the laundry down to the barn with no one noticing?" Nora could be seen to be thinking about it.

After several minutes passed, she shook her head no. Johannes looked satisfied with this, but asked, "Do you go into the laundry at night for any reason?" Nora nodded and said, "I help with the laundry at night after I finish washing up the dishes. I am usually in the laundry by two o'clock in the morning." Johannes and Jan were angry with themselves for not finding out who does the laundry sooner. Nora's answer made the two very excited and caused them to slide forward into their chairs.

"Nora, please be very sure of your answer before you answer my next question," emphasized Johannes. "What time were you in the laundry the morning the blood was found in the laundry? Please know you are not in any trouble." Nora looked over to Cornelia and saw a smile on her boss's face. "It is okay, dear, just answer their questions and everything will be okay," stated Cornelia. Nora fidgeted in her seat before answering. "I was in the laundry that morning at midnight. I was able to finish up with the dishes early because Cornelia had cleaned most of them after cooking."

As she looked to the floor, she continued with, "I did not see Antoon, the blood, or anything out of the normal."

Both the Brigadier and Inspector let out a sigh and thanked Nora for coming to see them. Cornelia stood up and walked out with Nora. Just as they left, Lars walked in with young Pieter de Jong. Pieter is twelve years old and works as the hall boy. Johannes gestured to them to have a seat and closed the door.

Lars introduced Pieter to the two policemen, "I want you to answer all of their questions. No matter your answer, you are not in trouble." Johannes repeated what Lars said about him not being in trouble, "We just hope you can help us answer some things we cannot figure out." Pieter was not like Nora; he is not shy or worried. He sat at the edge of the seat and quickly said, "If I can help with solving Antoon's murder, I want to. Antoon was like a big brother or… to me." Johannes leaned forward slightly. "You mean Antoon was like……a father to you?" Pieter nodded. "He helped me learn things, helped me with my chores, and he played games with me after work was done." Pieter became visibly upset but quickly settled himself.

Brigadier de Groot now had a situation that made him slightly uncomfortable. An orphan has adopted the murdered man as his father. Johannes asked, "How often did you go to Antoon's quarters?" Pieter shrugged his shoulders, "I woke him and the other male staff in the morning as one of my final tasks. I would fall asleep in his sitting room sometimes, but I would only be there when he was mainly." Johannes continued gently, "When was the last time you saw Antoon?" He became upset because he was sick and did not wake up the male staff that morning as usual. "Antoon put me to bed about midnight because I was vomiting. He finished my chores, and I fell asleep."

Lars was not aware of this. "Do you mean Antoon polished shoes, removed rubbish, and even took clean laundry up to the dressing rooms?" asked Lars. Pieter just nodded and looked down at the floor with tears in his eyes.

Pieter's rooms are on the same floor as the other staff members. Because of this, Antoon would have been walking around at night with Nora. "I wonder why Nora did not tell us you were sick that night," said Jan. Pieter look up and said, "We see little of each other at night, sir. Part of my duties take me up to the other floors of the palace."

"May I, gentlemen?" asked Lars. Both Johannes and Jan nodded. "Young man, did Antoon ever talk to you about the other staff, the family, or his time in London?" Pieter turned to his boss and replied, "I asked him about London, and he just said he was very busy. One weekend, he took me to Gouda to visit his mother. But we did not talk about palace things much." Jan turned to Johannes and gestured to the hallway.

As the two stood up, Jan said, "Please stay here. We will be back in a few moments." Jan led Johannes out to the hallway and closed the door behind them. Whispering, Jan asked, "This boy has adopted Antoon as his father, and it appears that Antoon adopted him as his son. I do not think we need to pressure this boy further, do you?" Johannes sighed and started stroking his beard. "You and I have some new information that we did not have before. First, we know Antoon was alive at midnight. Second, we know he was basically alone down here. He was also alive at two o'clock because he was not in the laundry when Nora was in there." Just as Johannes and Jan returned to the old cooks rooms, they overheard Lars tell Pieter, "I will send a letter to Antoon's mother, and I will let you know the answer as soon as I hear." Lars stood up and asked, "Do you gentlemen need anything further from us?"

Johannes and Jan shook their heads. Johannes stopped Lars just outside of the door. "What are you asking about Antoon's mother?" A smile came to his face that startled Johannes. "I am going to ask Antoon's mother if Pieter can live with her, sir. The young boy even calls her Oma, apparently."

Pieter's parents both died of pneumonia and influenza. At his five feet tall, he was shorter than most boys his age. Lars explained he was malnourished even in the orphanage. However, the previous Earl fed his staff very well. The stark blond hair and blue eyes were startling to see, thought Johannes.

Chapter

14

The following morning, Johannes was sitting in the old cook's rooms when Lars came to the door. "Brigadier, a letter has arrived for you, sir." As Lars handed Johannes the letter, he said, "I see it comes from the Koninklijke Marechaussee. Can I assume you are close to solving this, sir?" Johannes did not respond immediately. As Johannes read the letter, he responded, "I did not request information, but it looks like your footman told his mother some concerns."

Lars looked shocked and puzzled. Johannes allowed Lars to read the letter. The letter was from another investigator and said, "Brigadier de Groot, Antoon's mother, reports he verbalized some concerns. Unfortunately, she cannot remember who worried him. Also, when questioned if it relates to the palace or the London home, she could not recall. I have urged her to recall if he was worried about a male staffer or a female staffer, but she cannot recall much of anything other than he had concerns. All fingermarks appear to be in locations that one would expect, including the murder weapon. At this time, we cannot rule anyone out from the knife used to kill Meneer Antoon Mertens." As Lars finished reading, Daan and Jan stepped into the room.

"Gentlemen, I am not ashamed to admit that all the staff are worried." Lars handed the letter back to Johannes and continued. "I know Meneer Michael is recovering; however, the visible toll on the Earl and Countess is becoming more noticeable. Are you getting any closer? I am begging for an answer!"

Lars now has the facial expression to match the desperation in his voice. Johannes could not avoid this question. "Sir, I can say that I have my suspicions, and that this letter helps put some pieces together. I will know more after I meet with the family's old London staff." Johannes turned away for when Lars responded. "What is it I can do to help you, sir?" Johannes picked up his notebook. He wrote "Must meet with all Nassau London staff as soon as possible. Please have all report to the Palace Nassau immediately." As Johannes handed the note over, he asked Lars to have this telegram sent immediately. Lars nodded and walked over to his office to have it sent.

Johannes was now talking to Daan and Jan. "My friends, we are about to be very busy. Daan, may I rely on you to interview all the female staff? Jan, can you please interview the London outdoor staff? I will interview all the footmen, butler, and other male staff." Daan and Jan both nodded. "I will take the female staff to the room the boys call the Soestdijk Kammer," said Daan. Jan suggested he would use the servants' dining room. "I will interview the rest in here then," replied Johannes.

Lars returned after sending the telegram. "I took the liberty of telephoning the London home as well. The staff have moved to Lady Mary's father's estate. The estate is large enough to handle the extra staff."

"Thank you, Lars," replied Johannes from across the room. "Can we expect the staff to arrive soon?" Lars nodded, "I have been assured all of the London staff will arrive in two days. And before you ask, there are sixteen of them coming."

Daan stepped into the hall to give Lars his instructions, and to where the interviews will be conducted. Johannes and Jan walked up to Robert's study to update him. As they arrived, they found Robert and James sitting by the large fireplace. James appeared to be comforting his best friend. Michael and Charles were in the small library with their mothers and Willem.

Johannes knocked and waited to be invited in. "Come in" said Robert without looking up. Johannes and Jan bowed to the Earl and then the Duke once they were close. "My lord, I have been given information from the Koninklijke Marechaussee." Johannes handed the letter over and continued. "I am awaiting the arrival of the London staff; they will arrive in a couple of days." Robert and James read the letter when James asked, "Do you think this is related to London, then?" Before Johannes could even start to answer, Robert said, "Please sit down, gentlemen," and gestured to two empty chairs. "I cannot say one way or another, but I cannot ignore this letter and not interview them. I do not want to say yet, but this information is putting things together in my mind." Jan leaned forward so he could speak softly. "My lord, may I ask you a couple of questions about the London staff and your old position as a solicitor?" Robert nodded, and he drank some of his whiskey. "Were the London staff always the same? I mean, did you have anyone resign and replace anyone?" Robert had to think for several moments. "None of the male staff changed. You would need to ask my former butler about the others."

Jan nodded in understanding. He was now noticing what Lars mentioned about the toll being noticeable on the Earl's face. "As solicitor, did you have any incidents that could cause anything negative?" Robert shook his head. "I was mainly a consultant to members of Parliament, so I confirmed the legality of issues. I only did private law work for friends like the Duke and Duchess of Luxly, or family like my in-laws."

James shifted to turn to face Johannes and Jan more directly. "You do not think someone would kill a footman and kidnap my godson over legal fees, or some legal disputes?" James' face was that of anger, and his voice has a tone of disbelief. Nether Johannes or Jan could answer before Emma walked up to the four men. "Excuse me, My lord, I have a letter for you from the Prime Minister. It arrived just now by personal messenger."

Robert waved off Emma and opened the letter.

"Gentlemen, the Prime Minister is notifying me that the new political party in Germany is causing more military and political concerns across Europe. Apparently, my late father's suspicions of Germany are becoming more of a reality." Robert allowed the two policemen to read the letter. "Could this be the reason for the attempt on my son, and Antoon's death is a separate situation?" Johannes shook his head even before Robert finished his question.

"My lord, Antoon's murder is related to the attempt on Meneer Michael. I am never wrong, my lord, and the Inspector can confirm this." Jan nodded with a slight smirk. "He has never been wrong, my lord." Johannes stood, "May we be excused, my lord? We need to prepare for the other interviews." Robert and James both stood and shook both of the policemen's hands. As James shook Johannes' hand, he asked, "How long will this take, sir?"

After clearing his throat and attempting to watch his own facial expression, Johannes answered. "My last case took three months, your grace. And that case was the stolen Van Gogh from a private collection in Amsterdam. I am aware of the urgency, but pressing me will not make it progress faster."

As the Brigadier closed the doors, Jan smirked. "I do not think His Grace approved of your facial responce, my friend." Johannes turned to the Inspector, "You know how I do not respond well to being pushed or questioned." Jan recognizes the look Johannes has now.

"You have everything solved in your mind, and I know better than to even ask." Johannes did not even look to Jan when he replied, "I just need to prove everything, and I think we are close to that."

Johannes, in fact, knows everything but needs to have more confirmation. Once they returned to their temporary quarters, Johannes settled into one of the armchairs. Daan asked, "How did that go?" Johannes turned to the Inspector and Major Dekker. "After the interviews, I will review the evidence and timelines with you both." Jan had to answer Dekker's question, "I do not think the Duke appreciated the Brigadiers' responses, but the Earl appears to be one of understanding."

Lars knocked on the door. "Come in," announced Dekker. Lars was carrying a large tea tray with snacks for the policemen. "The London staff should arrive on Friday morning. Is there anything that you will need?" Johannes was directly across from Dekker, close to the fireplace. "Please have a seat and join us for a moment, Lars," suggested Dekker.

Jan got himself some tea and biscuits and leaned back into his chair. "I understand that the London butler is now the under butler at Lady Mary's father's country estate. Do you know much else of the London staff?" asked Jan.. Lars picked up some tea before responding. "Lady Mary's father's country estate is large enough to support the extra staff, from my understanding. His estate supplies all the grains and feeds for the Royal stables and a whiskey maker in Scotland." Dekker looked over to Johannes to see him stroking that beard of his again. "Did your Antoon ever talk about his time with the London staff?" asked Dekker. Lars nodded. "He telephoned me or Bram daily to give updates on the move, instructions by their lordships, or to notify when personal items and furniture would arrive." Jan wrote a few notes before asking his last question. "Did Antoon talk about any of the staff specifically?" Lars thought for several minutes before responding, "Only mentioned the movers were making some of the female staff uncomfortable. Apparently, there was a moving man pinching their posteriors and making comments about the Great War while moving furniture and other items."

Johannes stopped mid-stroke of his beard. "Do we have this mover's name or company information?" Johannes did not even turn his head from looking at the mantel clock when asking. Lars shook his head and set down the teacup, and replied, "The London butler should remember that information. It was a Dutch company that collected it from the harbor and delivered it here." The clock on the mantel chimed to announce one o'clock.

A smirk reappeared on Johannes's face, and he resumed stroking his beard. "Lars, would you be opposed to sitting in on the interviews of the male staff with me?" Johannes's question stunned both Dekker and Jan. "How would I be of help, sir?" asked Lars. "You have an attention to detail that others do not have. My colleagues will interview the other staff, and I need your level of observation." A look of realization and understanding appeared on Jan's face.

"Lars, the Brigadier wants you to be a professional witness in other words. You are an expert in running a home and would know if their actions or answers are appropriate."

Daan shuffled himself into his armchair. "I am not comfortable with that idea, Brigadier," announced the Major. "My dear Major," Johannes is now using his commanding voice, "Lars is not connected with the murder or the attempted kidnapping of Michael. I have cleared him in all aspects of this case. I need his experience, as the Inspector explained. Lars has my full trust!" Johannes is now looking directly at Major Daan Dekker with the look that no one could deny was that of his confidence. Brigadier Johannes de Groot has a reputation with the Rijkspolitie and Koninklijke Marechaussee of becoming angry when not being listened to or when questioned. Daan's body language changed immediately with the glare from Johannes. At that moment, Lars knew that he would be attending the interviews if he wanted to or not.

That Friday morning, the clock in the cook's rooms chimed nine o'clock, and the bell at the servants' doors rang. "That will be the other staff, Brigadier. Shall I let them in and direct them to the rooms?" Johannes nodded as Daan and Jan walked out with Lars. "This is the day I will know everything," thought Johannes.

As Lars opened the door, he greeted George, the butler from the London home. "Afternoon, he greeted everyone. If the male house staff will follow me to the servant's hall outside the staff dining hall. Major Dekker and Inspector Jansen will direct the others."

Lars walked the butler, footmen, and the hall boy down the hallway and directed them to sit in the chairs set out for them. "I will take all the female staff upstairs through here," as he points to the servant's staircase. Jan looked and only aw four outdoor staff members waiting for him. "I will meet with you in the dining hall. would you please follow me?" Jan directed the four to sit in the chairs by the other male staff. "I will be with you momentarily," he announced as he walked into the dining hall. Johannes never left the temporary quarters or his armchair.

Lars walked in without knocking, "Sir, who would you like to meet with first?" Johannes never turned around. "I will let you decide that, Lars." If Johannes was looking, he would have seen a smirk develop across Lars' face. "I will ask George to come in first, sir," as he walked out. Lars returned with George, and Johannes was now sitting at the end of the table.

The Brigadier gestured to Lars to sit on the opposite side of the table, with George across from him. George, knowing who the Brigadier is, bowed to the Knight Grand Cross.

The moment the two butlers sat, Johannes spoke up. "George, I am going to have Lars talk and ask you questions." At this moment, Lars turned to face the Brigadier in disbelief. Johannes continued, "I will sit here listening and taking notes. If there are questions at the end, I will add mine to his. Do you understand, sir?" George nodded, "Yes, ridder de Groot." The now flustered butler, Lars, took a couple of moments to devise the questions he felt the police would what to know. "George, do you remember the name of the moving company or any of the movers at the London home?" George pulled out a small black diary and opened it to the last few pages. He fingered over page by page until he stopped. "There were two moving companies used. The first on the English side, and then one on the Dutch side. Wright Moving and Shipping with a London address. The owner is Albert Wright, and here is his information."

After he writes the information and handed it to Lars, he continued. "Peeters Moving in Rotterdam was used on this side of the move. The owner is Gijs Peeters and here is his information." George finished up and handed Lars that information.

Lars told his counterpart about the mover Antoon told him made some female staff uncomfortable. As Lars spoke, George was nodding. George was turning the pages of his diary to 12th of May 1920. "On the 12th of May, I called Wright Moving and Shipping and ordered that they remove……an Alexander Smyth from this move." Lars wrote the name and the date. George continued, "I had several staff members, including male staff, complain about Mr. Smyth. He made several people uncomfortable because he was talking about the Great War, how the Great Families will not be so great in the future, and also made some fascist comments. Your Antoon Mertens assisted me in escorting Mr. Smyth out of the London home." This made the Brigadier sit up and lean forward. Lars looked to Johannes, but the Brigadier gestured for Lars to continue.

Lars continued as instructed. "Was anything else out of place that you can recall?" George shook his head. "That was the only thing out of routine." Lars looks at the list of the London staff. "Do you think any of these staff members would have any information that would help the police?" George shook his head no. "I know all of us want to help the Earl and Countess, but we especially want to help Meneer Michael."

Lars looked over to the Brigadier as he asked George, "Is there anything left in the London home that belonged to the Earl, Countess, or Meneer Michael?" George thought for a few moments and then shook his head no. "What the family did not bring here, they kept in the London home for the Countess Nassau's father." Suddenly, George stood up like a shot. "Gentlemen, I just remembered that there was a break in the day after the family left for the Netherlands." Johannes stood up and walked over to George. "I hope you contacted the police, sir." George nodded and turned his diary to another page. He wrote the Constable's name and handed it directly to the Brigadier. After all the interviews were completed, the three policemen sat and compared notes.

As Johannes explained the break-in at the London home, Dekker offered to travel to London. Johannes shook his head and commanded that he would not only go to London, but he will also go to Delft. "Daan, what did you find in Breda?" asked Johannes with a sharp tone. Daan pulled out his notes. "I have confirmed that Tess's and Emma's credentials are correct. Emma's brother does, in fact, own a bakery in Old Breda square." Johannes continued, "Did you talk to her brother, or did you just clarify through the Netherlands Defense Academy?" Daan did not like the accusations from Johannes, but he only clarified through the academy. Johannes stood up and walked out of the room. Both the Major and Inspector just sat there looking at each other, knowing that the Brigadier is not in a good mood. A few minutes later, Johannes returned and went into the sleeping room.

Chapter
15

George and Lars came to the old cook's quarters with a sense of duty about them. "Sir, I have been instructed to take you to the London home and make you comfortable," stated George. Johannes turned to face George and noticed a look about him that made it clear this was an order by the Earl. "His lordship will not be in the London home for two weeks; Parliament is not in session this week. I have been instructed to settle you in a guest room and provide your meals and anything you may require."

Mary's father was a bit of a snob, even for British aristocracy standards, but Johannes is the highest-ranking knight in the Dutch kingdom. So, in the Earl's eyes, Johannes is an equal and will be treated with the highest standards.

Johannes stood from the armchair and turned towards Lars. "Could you please contact the Rijkspolitie and arrange for transportation for me to London first thing tomorrow?" George took a step forward. "The Earl has arranged transportation for you and I to London. We leave House Nassau at six o'clock in the morning, and we will arrive at the London house just after midday in two days. Also, I am to hand this directly to Countess Nassau. George pulled an envelope from his pocket." Johannes thanked George and excused him and Lars for completing that task.

Each of the London staff have been provided with sleeping arrangements in the palace.

After George delivered Mary's father's note to her, he requested an audience with Robert. "My lord, I have been tasked to take de hoogwelgeboren heer Johannes ridder de Groot to the London home tomorrow. The Earl wished I ask you to read this and take it into consideration." George pulled out a similar envelope that he gave Mary.

As George and Lars leave Robert's study, Mary and Robert began reading their letters. A smile appears on Mary's face as her father's letter reminded her of his kindness and love. Robert, however, read the letter from his father-in-law with some hesitation.

"My dear boy, I understand how difficult these days must be. I advise you to celebrate the life of Michael and his safety with an early birthday calibration. I know you may not feel this is appropriate, but I strongly suggest that you and Mary celebrate."

At five thirty in the morning, Johannes was ready to leave for London. Both the Major and Inspector were still sleeping. As Johannes locked the door behind him, George and Lars greeted him. "Good morning, sir, we have a car waiting for us outside the staff door," and George took the Brigadier's luggage. Cornelia met the Brigadier by the door, holding sacks of food. "I have packed food for you and George for your trip, sir. I know the ship will have food, but you will need this on the train." Brigadier Johannes de Groot thanked Cornelia and walked to the awaiting car.

The two-day journey gave Johannes the time and space to compile all the information he has collected. George escorted Johannes to his rooms in the London house and asked, "Would you like your lunch in your room or in the small dining room, sir?" Johannes requested to have his lunch and dinner in his room if that was not too much trouble. George gave the Brigadier a bow and left.

By one of the windows, Johannes sat in a tall leather wingback chair with a footstool. Next to the chair, he moved a small table to the right side of the chair to be a makeshift desk. As Johannes stroked his thick beard, he closed his eyes. A short while later, a house maid delivered a fully stocked food tray and sat it in front of the Knight. She gave a quick bow and excused herself. "Just a moment please," announced Johannes. "Yes, my lord," replied the housemaid. "Are you a regular house maid here? "No, my lord, I am here from the Earl's estate while you are in London," replied the maid. She continued, "The staff will remain in the Netherlands for another day, I understand." Johannes ate one of the best meals he has ever had. Once full, he took out a brand- new notebook and pencil. As Johannes organized his thoughts into his book, along with evidence, facts, lies, and other pertinent information, George knocked on the door. "What can I do to assist you, my lord?" asked George. "I need to go to the moving company first thing in the morning." George bowed and made those arrangements.

By the time George returned, Johannes was not in his room. The Brigadier took it upon himself to walk around all the rooms in the London house. He made note of the rooms he thought belonged to the Earl and Countess, Meneer Michael, and even looked through the staff rooms. By the time he returned to his room, he found the dinner tray with a note.

"My lord, I have arranged for the motorcar to take you to Wright Moving and Shipping at ten o'clock in the morning. The Constable that came to the break-in will be here to answer your questions at six o'clock tomorrow evening. Please do not hesitate to pull the bell cord if you need anything further."

Johannes finished the meal and returned to the tall chair. With all of his notes in hand, he fell asleep. It was the sunrise coming through the windows the following morning that woke him up. "If this case does not kill me, I will retire when I am done", he thought as he prepared himself for the day.

In front of the Wright Moving and Shipping company, Albert Wright met Johannes. "My lord, I have been told to expect your arrival," greeted Mr. Wright. He continued, "I will hopefully be able to help you with what you need, sir. Please come into my office."

Albert Wright was a short and lean man. Johannes noted he was pale and possibly Irish, or maybe even Scottish. His suit was clean, but was not fitted well to him. Mr. Wright sat next to the Brigadier in a large office. He handed the documents from the Nassau move to Johannes. "You will note that the day, time, payment information, number of items, and a detailed inventory are there. On the last page, my lord, you will find the names of the crew on the job." Mr. Wright continued; Scotland Yard reached out to my company on your behalf." Johannes nodded. "They could clear everyone's name… except Alexander Smyth." Johannes nodded again. "I have a feeling that it is an alias."

Johannes continued to look through the documents, and Mr. Wright handed one last paper over to the investigator. "This is the address, name, and other information that Alexander Smyth gave my company when he was hired. The man who hired him is no longer employed here, either." Johannes requested to interview the other members of the moving crew, and Mr. Wright made the arrangements.

Once Johannes completed meeting the other movers, he took the chauffeured car back to the London house. George greeted him and walked him into the large library where the Constable was waiting for him. "I am very sorry for being late, sir. I was delayed at the moving company," said Johannes. The Constable bowed. "I am just honored to help you, my lord. The butler informed me you are interested in the break-in reported the day after the Earl and his family left for the Netherlands." Johannes nodded and sat next to the Constable.

Constable Baker was what Johannes expected for a young, fit Constable. Blond hair and dark brown eyes could deceive you to think he was older than his 20 years. The London Police uniform was spotless, and even to the point that Johannes could see attention to detail. "I bet it would be painful for him to be untidy," Johannes thought.

As the Constable handed the file over, the Brigadier was impressed by what he saw. "This is very well put together, constable." The report detailed the forced staff door below stairs, disturbed furniture in the library, bedrooms, and even in the butler's office. Johannes asked, "Was anything reported missing?" The Constable shook his head. "Apparently the staff could do an inventory quickly because of the recent move by the family." The Constable continued, "There were finger marks collected, and we have a file on an Alexander Smyth.

He has been arrested for disturbances and assault." Johannes took out the report from Scotland Yard and showed the Constable that even they feel that was an alias and not his real name. "I have arrested him myself, sir, for assault."

Johannes turned. "What does his voice sound like?" The Constable thought for a moment. "His accent is like yours, my lord, but his was more pronounced." Johannes thought a moment. "Do you think he is Dutch?" The Constable shook his head no. "I have met the Earl Nassau, and now hearing your accent, like the Earl's, I do not think it was a Dutch accent."

"Can you please have your supervisor come here, Constable?" asked Johannes. A confused look came across the Constable's face. "I need you to be assigned to me temporarily and come back to the Netherlands. I have a plan that I need your help with," explained Johannes. The Constable telephoned his police station and handed the receiver over to the Brigadier.

After several minutes, Johannes announced, "It is arranged. You will travel to the Netherlands in a couple of days. I will return tomorrow. Here is the address that you need to report to, and I will not accept tardiness. You will be briefed by myself, Major Daan Dekker, and Inspector Jan Jansen." Constable Henry Baker bowed and excused himself.

George walked into the library. "My lord, may I ask why you need a British Constable?" Johannes continued walking but answered, "He is the only one of us that has spoken to him besides yourself and Antoon. I need him to help identify Alexander Smyth safely." By the time Johannes finished his response, he was at the top of the stairs.

The following day, Johannes was thinking about how Antoon visited someone in Delft regularly. "Would Antoon tell them who concerned him in London?" thought Johannes as he stepped onto the train. As he sat down in the seat, he was the only one in that train car. On a small piece a paper, the Brigadier looked over the address on Oude Delft written with Thijs Phillips written.

Thijs was a military friend, Antoon visited in Delft regularly. The London butler was to the same standards as Lars in Johannes' opinion. Between the two butlers, Johannes could get more information about Thijs than anyone in the Rijkspolitie. The Brigadier laughed to himself after thinking, "Maybe I should start recommending recruiting from butlers for the Rijkspolitie for now on."

George would make sure that he and the young constable would make it to House Nassau in time. Johannes had complete trust in George and Lars at this point. The Brigadier even left money for George and Constable Baker to have food for the voyage.

The long train ride allowed Johannes to relax. This was the first time since he was called into this case that he felt relaxed. The rhythmic clacking of the train on the tracks put Johannes to sleep for the last three hours of the train ride. Once in Delft, Johannes only had a five-minute walk to his destination.

Thijs' house was a typical canal house in a historic city. It has a stone façade with dark green window shutters with a matching door. After several unanswered knocks, Johannes found a cafe and try again after eating. The Nieuwe Kirk's bell announced eleven o'clock, and he followed the chimes to the old square.

Just across the oude stadhuis in Delft was a nice cafe with several outdoor seating options. After eating a light midday meal, Johannes walked back to find Thijs at home.

"May I speak with you, sir? I am Brigadier de Groot with the Rijkspolitie." Thijs looked Johannes up and down and looked over the Brigadier's credentials. "Is this regarding Antoon's death, sir?" Johannes nodded. "I just have a few questions if that is alright, sir. I apologize for any inconvenience." Thijs opened the door further and gestured for him to enter. Thijs' house was originally a pottery business with apartments above, but has since been converted to a house.

A five-meter-tall ceiling greeted Johannes with a massive fireplace. A kitchen with a table and chairs was in front of the main windows, that were floor to ceiling.

"Please have a seat, de hoogwelgeboren heer." The butlers have clearly made Thijs aware of Johannes' title. "Please call me Brigadier for now, sir. I understand you were close with Antoon." Thijs placed a cup of coffee in front of Johannes, then sat across from him. "Antoon and I served in the military together during the great war, but went to school together as boys in Gouda." Johannes did not even take out his notebook. He was looking around the house and noted Thijs was a bachelor and had little more than the necessities. "Did Antoon ever talk to you about concerns he had at work or while he was in London with Lord Nassau's family?" A blank look came across Thijs' face. He was not aware of the cause of death of his friend."

A few moments passed without an answer from Thijs. Antoon was murdered at House Nassau in Zuid-

Holland province. I think he was murdered to keep him quiet from disclosing information." Thijs noticeably became uncomfortable and shifted in his chair.

"I…I was told he was killed, but was not told how or when. His mother wrote to me to tell me she wanted me to come to Gouda to help arrange his funeral."

Johannes sat back in the chair slightly and drank some of the coffee. "What can you tell me about your friend?" Thijs smiled. "He was the greatest friend any man or woman could have. He cared deeply for his family and friends. He took his job for the Nassau family extremely seriously and held pride in his position. He would never discuss private matters or go into much about work." Johannes was not happy with that response; he hoped Thijs would have a name or place that concerned Antoon. Thijs continued, "He would do anything to help someone in need. Even if he was busy, he would offer to help others."

"Did he ever mention going to London to help the Earl and Countess move?" Thijs nodded. "He stayed the night here and took the train out of Delft the following morning.

After spending the time in London, he returned here on his way to Gouda. But he mentioned no concerns, he was his happy normal self both visits."

Johannes drank the last of his coffee and asked his final question. "Did Antoon have anyone special in his life?" Thijs shook his head and took the cup away from Johannes. "We both have been bachelor's our entire lives. I guess that is why I appreciated my friendship with him so much." Just before Johannes walked out, he asked one last question as he turned back to face Thijs. "Do you have any of Antoon's belongings here?" This question apparently shocked Thijs with his facial response. "No, sir, he was only here once in a while." Johannes thanked Thijs and walked to the Delft station.

The Brigadier replayed everything he learned in his mind over and over as he traveled by train. His gut was telling him something, but he was not sure what it was saying yet. He knew he would have the difficult task of asking the Prime Minister for a favor. He took out a piece of notepaper and jotted down a quick note. Just before getting onto the train, he suddenly changed his mind.

Chapter 16

Now sitting on the train going to Gouda, Antoon's mother will be the last bit of the puzzle needed to prove the Brigadier's case. Johannes sat on the train, knowing that he needs to help Antoon's mother to remember what Antoon told her. With Pieter at the back of the brigadier's mind, he knew this would be an extra sensitive meeting.

As Johannes walked past the Gouda Stadhuis, he was thinking about the questions he would ask Mirjam Mertens. He knew well that Antoon did, in fact, talk to his mother about some concerns he had. Just as the bells chimed at Saint John Church, the Brigadier stopped in his tracks. "I know who killed Antoon, and I know who took Michael. I just need help to prove it," he said out loud. Johannes de Groot stood in front of the five-hundred-year-old house where Antoon grew up. Through the front window, he could see Mirjam sitting in a chair, reading a book.

Just as he reached up to knock on the front door, Thijs Phillips walked up to the Brigadier. "I had a feeling you would come here next, sir; I think I should be here to make Mevrouw Mertens more comfortable." Just as Thijs finished, Mirjam was looking out the window at the two men. "The door is unlocked, Thijs, please come in, both of you," announced Mirjam.

Thijs hugged Mirjam and sat down in the sitting room. "This is Brigadier de hoogwelgeboren heer Johannes ridder de Groot," Thijs explained, he was investigating.

Antoon's murder and Meneer Michaels kidnapping. Mirjam nodded to Johannes and gestured to have him sit. "I can make us some tea or coffee if you would like," stated Mirjam. "I can do that, mevrouw," responded Thijs as he stood and walked into the kitchen. Mirjam looked at Johannes for a few minutes before asking, "Are you here to see if I can remember what my son told me about his concerns?" Johannes only nodded. "Before I answer your questions, I have one for you, sir." Johannes slid closer to the edge of the seat and sat up even straighter. "How may I be of help to you, Mevrouw Mertens?" Mirjam took a letter out of her book and handed it over to the Brigadier. "Do you know anything about this?" asked Mirjam.

It was the letter from Lars about the young Pieter de Jong. "I only learned about him recently," stated Johannes. Mirjam reached out to take the letter back. "My son was in love, but I do not know who won his heart. He never had children of his own, but this Pieter became my Antoon's son and my grandson. I will take the young man in because I know that is what

Antoon would want, and I also want it. Pieter will have Antoon's childhood room."

At this moment, Thijs walked in holding a tray of tea, cups, and some biscuits. "I hope this is okay, Mevrouw Mertens," announced Thijs as he set the tray down. "Well done, Thijs," agreed Mirjam. "I knew about Pieter, Brigadier, but it was not my place to tell you. Antoon and Pieter have been to see me at Delft several times. Pieter loved Antoon as a father, and Antoon loved Pieter as a son." Thijs continued, "I promise not to hold anything further from you, sir." Johannes turned to Thijs and asked, "Is there anything else you would like to tell me?" Thijs simply looked ashamed and responded, "No, sir."

Johannes took a few moments to observe the house that Antoon grew up in. It is one of the older homes of Gouda and looked like it was professionally cleaned. Johannes thought, "The detail for cleanliness and a place for everything must come from Antoon's mother." One of the walls in the sitting room was covered with books of all ages and several languages.

Photos of Antoon and what looked to be his father were placed in nice rows. The floor to ceiling windows filled the ground floor with light. That light landed on Mirjam's sad face, showing that she was still grieving for her son.

"One of your colleagues came to see me. He asked me about my Antoon and how he confided in me about some concerns he had." Mirjam continued after taking a drink of tea. "How did you know my son had concerns?" Johannes took a couple sips of good tea and replied with, "Your son had a piece paper in his rooms at the palace that suggested he wrote to my colleagues in Koninklijke Marechaussee." Mirjam was nodding at this point, "I advised my son to do that, Brigadier." She continued with, "Is that the reason my son was murdered?" Johannes simply shrugged his shoulders; he did not want to make her feel responsible.

Johannes was getting more curious, but he did not want to push this grieving mother. "Do you know what Antoon's father and I did as a profession, Brigadier?" Mirjam leaned forward and had a slight smile on her face.

"My husband was a scientist that worked for the Kingdom of the Netherlands, and I was a nurse. My late husband died of influenza. His pension and position with the government allowed me to remain home with Antoon as a child." Thijs spoke up, "I grew up next door," as he pointed to the house he grew up in. "My parents are both still living, fortunately, but Mevrouw Mirjam was always like a second mother to me." Thijs took it upon himself to help Johannes break the difficult question to Mirjam. "Can you remember who Antoon said he was worried about?" Johannes was relieved that he was not the one to break the silence. "I know Antoon came home after being in London. He told me that there was a mover making fascist comments, making comments about the great families of Europe not being great for long, and making comments about the Great War.

Antoon and Thijs served our kingdom during the great

war, and I know he was not happy about that man. He continued to say that he would make inappropriate gestures to the female staff." Johannes leaned forward and asked, "Did he comment about anyone at House Nassau?" Mirjam could be seen to think, but shook her head.

Mirjam stood up, "Brigadier, do you want to see Antoon's room? He has many of his things from childhood and adulthood in there." Johannes stood and thanked her. "I will take him up, mevrouw," offered Thijs. Antoon's best friend led the Brigadier up the stairs to Antoon's room. A single-person bed at the side of the room was made and ready for Antoon to show up for his next visit. The chest of drawers and wardrobe were at the opposite side of the bed.

Thijs opened up the wardrobe and sorted through Antoon's clothing. Johannes was looking through the bedside table and found a piece of paper with Antoon's writing on it. "Koninklijke Marechaussee" was written on it with the Den Haag address below it. Just below the address, "Alexander Smyth" was written down.

"Thijs," barked Johannes, making Thijs jump. "Yes, sir?" he quickly responded. "Did Antoon ever say the name Alexander Smyth, or a variation of that name, to you?" Thijs sat on Antoon's bed next to the Brigadier. "Sir, I have never heard that name before. Is it English?" Johannes handed the paper over to Thijs and replied, "I think it is a fake name used by someone who broke into the London home and was a mover that caused your best friend to be concerned."

As the two were going through Antoon's papers and personal items, Mirjam walked in. "Do you think Pieter will enjoy this room?" Thijs spoke up before Johannes had the chance. "I know Pieter will just be happy to live in the room his father grew up in." Mirjam smiled and walked back to the sitting room. Johannes turned to Thijs. "That was the right thing to say."

When Johannes and Thijs made it back to the ground floor, they noticed an amazing smell of food. "Come in here, boys and sit down to eat," announced Mirjam from the dining room. Mirjam had made stamppot for them to eat. "I want to feed the man who will find my son's killer," said Mirjam as she sat down. The meal with Mirjam and Thijs provided more information about Antoon.

An hour later, Thijs drove the Brigadier to the train station. "Sir, I hope you now have everything that you need to end this." Johannes closed the door and replied, "I know what I need to do."

"Oh…. Brigadier, can you please give this to young Pieter please?" Thijs grabbed a suitcase from the back and handed it to Johannes. Mirjam wanted Pieter to have some of Antoon's clothing from when he was his age.

Johannes smiled and said, "I will make sure he gets these when I return." Thijs watched as the Brigadier got onto the train to The Hague.

Chapter 17

Johannes walked over to Robert's study immediately after his arrival. Robert was sitting at the desk, working on some paperwork.

Michael and Charles were on the other side, playing chess. Willem was standing guard between the boys and the Earl, keeping an eye on each window and door. Johannes was looking for the Prime Minister, but he was not in the study. Johannes did not want to be noticed and could walk by unnoticed, except by Willem. Willem simply nodded with a smile to the Brigadier to acknowledge his intention.

Bram was walking toward Johannes from the large portrait hallway. Johannes held up his large hand to stop Bram and whispered, "I am looking for the Prime Minister. I understand he is working here today." Bram nodded and guided Johannes to the Royal Delft room. As the two walked down the grand hallway, they passed four uniformed and armed policemen.

Without knocking, Johannes entered the room and quickly closed the door behind him. The Prime Minister was working at a small desk in the corner. The Royal Delft room was lined with white and blue silk walls.

A large gold and crystal chandelier centered the room. Cabinets filled with new and antique Royal Delft porcelain filled the walls. Several tables had Royal Delft centerpieces scattered around the room. The grand fireplace even has Royal Delft tile on it.

"I am sorry, Prime Minister, but I must speak to you in private." The Prime Minister turned and held his hand out, directing him to the chair next to him. "How may I be of help, Brigadier?"

As the Brigadier sat down, he spoke softly. "I need to get an audience with Queen Wilhelmina." The expression on the Prime Minister's face was unchanged. He pulled out some paper and a fountain pen from his briefcase.

As the Prime Minister unscrewed the cap to his pen, he asked, "What day shall I request, and for what reason?" Johannes pulled out a note from his suit jacket and handed it to the Prime Minister. The look of surprise fell onto the Prime Minister's face. "Well, that complicates things or simplifies them," replied the Prime Minister as he placed the cap back onto his pen. He picked up the telephone receiver and waited for the operator. "I need the secretary to the Queen; this is the Prime Minister calling from Palace Nassau."

A few moments passed, and he was connected with Het Loo Palace in Apeldoorn. Johannes could only hear one side of the conversation. The Prime Minister informed the secretary, "It is a matter of the most importance that de hoogwelgeboren heer Johannes ridder de Groot sees Her Majesty tomorrow." The Prime Minister dropped the Brigadier's police title and used his knighthood title instead.

After he replaced the telephone receiver, the Prime Minister looked to Johannes. "Her Majesty will meet you tomorrow at one o'clock at Het Loo." Johannes stood and shook his hand. As he turned to walk away, he stopped about halfway. "What does one wear when meeting the Queen of your country for this particular reason?" The Prime Minister smiled, "A fresh dark suit and hat will be fine, sir."

Johannes took the back servants' staircase. At the bottom, he found Bram reading a newspaper while drinking his tea. He was sitting in the staff dining hall alone. "Sir, I need your help again," as he stood next to Bram. "How may I be of help, Brigadier?" Johannes cleared his throat. "I am needing my dress uniform freshened up. Any chance you could help me? By the looks of your own uniform, you are the one to ask." Bram almost blushed at this compliment, "Thank you sir, I will be happy to assist you with that." As he walked away, he remembered the suitcase. "Oh, can you get the small suitcase out of my motorcar? There are Antoon's childhood clothing in it for Pieter." Bram smiled, "I will be happy to, sir. I think Pieter needs that right now."

Johannes gave his dress uniform and shoes over to Bram. The Major and the Inspector looked to Johannes with some confusion. Dekker stood. "Why do you need your dress uniform?" As Johannes took a cup and poured some tea, as he announced, "I am going to Apeldoorn in the morning." Inspector Jansen whistled, followed by, "You are getting an audience with Her Majesty." Jansen did not ask; he simply made the statement, knowing Johannes would not explain further.

About an hour passed, and Bram returned with the uniform and shoes. "My good man, the uniform looks like new!" Johannes exclaimed with his compliments. Bram handed them over and replied, "The fifth footman will arrive with coffee and pastries for you, gentlemen." Johannes thanked Bram again and hung the uniform up on the wall hook. Bram continued, "Pieter, thanks you for Antoon's clothing. Some trousers are too large, but Fleur said she would hem them."

Upstairs, Michael was in bed but not able to sleep. Something in the palace felt off to him again. When he sleeps, he has nightmares about the man who attempted to kidnap him. He cannot place the voice or even the accent still.

Charles was sound asleep in the bed next to him, and he was sure Willem was asleep as well. Michael's mantel clock chimed at eleven o'clock, but he just stared up at the carved wood ceiling in his room. A few moments passed when he heard one of the policemen talking to another man in the hallway. "Must be time to change shifts," he thought to himself.

"The Brigadier must be getting closer to solving this

case," one of the policemen said in the hallway. Michael got out of the bed and walked over to the locked door to his room. "The Brigadier is getting closer for sure; he is getting ready to meet with Her Majesty in the morning."

After Michael heard this, a slight sensation of comfort came over him, but just slightly. No longer able to hear the policemen talking, Michael went over to the armchairs next to his large windows. Looking out the center window, there was just enough light to see the policemen stationed outside the palace doors. Michael looked back to his friend and noticed that Charles was now awake.

"What is wrong?" asked Charles. "When I sleep, I can hear his voice," replied Michael softly. Charles walked over and sat next to his friend. As Charles looked out the window, he sees three uniform policemen standing at the door. "I do not think anyone can attempt anything with these policemen around." Michael did not respond to his friend's comment.

Willem walked into Michael's room. "Is there something wrong, boys?" Michael kept looking out his window. Charles walked over to Willem, "He cannot sleep. He said he hears his voice when he sleeps." Willem nodded in understanding and patted Charles' shoulder.

Charles could see a genuine look of concern on Willem's face. Willem walked over to Michael. "Your father is working late tonight. Shall we go down?" Michael looked up, and Willem could see tears coming down

Michael's face. "Take me to father, please."

As Michael and Charles put on their dressing gowns, Willem unlocked the hidden passage door. "We will take this down to your father's study." The three walked down the passage with Willem leading. Once Willem opened the passage into the study, you could hear Robert typing. All three stepped through to see Robert at his desk and hearing the clacking of the typewriter getting louder. James was sleeping on the sofa by the fireplace. Just as Charles stays close to his best friend, his father does the same with his.

"My lord, Meneer Michael cannot sleep," Willem whispered to not bother the sleeping Duke. "He is having nightmares related to the incident," he continued. Robert stopped typing, "Come here, my boy, pull up a chair next to me." Michael did as his father instructed and pulled an oversized leather armchair next to him and climbed into it. "The two of you should go back to bed. Leave the passage unlocked, and I will lock it when I bring Michael up later. The study doors are locked from the inside, Willem." Willem walked over to Robert and handed him a pistol, "Do you know how to use this, my lord?" Robert nodded and placed it next to him on his desk opposite Michael. Michael put his head on his father's shoulder and closed his eyes. "I will take the Marquess up," said Willem as he guided Charles back to the hidden door. Charles looked back to his friend as they walked through, and Willem pulled it closed behind them. "He needs to be with his father, and you and I need to get some sleep," said Willem as he yawned.

Robert returned to his work, and Michael could sleep without nightmares. The tall clock in the study chimed two o'clock, and Robert picked up his only child and carried him up to his room through the passage. Robert walked through and tapped on the small door connecting into Willem's room. "Willem, here is this back," as he replaced the pistol next to Willem on his bedside table. "I will go back through the passage and lock the doors behind me."

The Brigadier woke before anyone else the following morning. After dressing in his dress uniform, he walked out the staff door at the side of the palace. He did not want to be noticed to be leaving, and he needed to stop in The Hague on his way to Apeldoorn. Once in Apeldoorn, Johannes could feel his stomach in his throat. He stopped at a small café for his morning meal and some coffee. He was not the type to show fear or apprehension, but the waiter noticed the look on Johannes' face. "Extra coffee, sir?" asked the waiter. Johannes accepted quickly.

After finishing his meal and coffee, Johannes returned to his motorcar. As the Brigadier approached the gates to Het Loo, the feeling of apprehension grew.

Het Loo is the residence of the Dutch Monarch, and Oranje-Nassau is the house of Queen Wilhelmina. The Brigadier was about to enter the palace and ask the Queen for a personal favor and a task that could be found impertinent. "This is necessary," he thought out loud as he drove up to the gates.

The Koninklijke Marechaussee saluted Johannes as he

drove up. After confirming his appointment, he was granted access through the large, grand gates. The lump in his throat grew larger as he got closer to the palace. Johannes was well aware of the significance of the palace and the task before him. The butler and the Queen's secretary greeted Johannes at the palace entrance and bowed to him. "De hoogwelgeboren heer Johannes ridder de Groot, Her Majesty, will meet you in her study." The secretary gestured to Johannes to follow him up the grand staircase.

Johannes has spent several days at Palace Nassau, but he is more aware of the significance of Het Loo now that he is there. Silk-lined walls, massive chandeliers, portraits of Kings and Queens, as well as plush carpets as far as he could see. The Brigadier felt out of place just as he was directed to sit on a gilded chair in the massive hallway. "Please sit here, sir; I will announce you to Her Majesty." The secretary disappeared through a massive, gilded doorway.

Johannes could now feel his heart pounding inside of his chest, and it skipped a beat as the secretary reappeared. "Her Majesty will see you now." Johannes stood and immediately felt lightheaded, and his mouth watered like he was going to be sick.

As he stepped into the room, the Brigadier's focus landed on Queen Wilhelmina. Her kind face caused a calm to rush over him. Johannes bowed, "Your majesty, thank you for granting me this meeting." As his voice cracked, the Queen smiled to calm him even more. "Brigadier de Groot, I understand you are leading the investigation at my cousins. Is that the reason for our meeting?" Johannes took a breath. "It is your majesty."

"I am pleased to see you again, but not under these circumstances," replied the Queen. Queen Wilhelmina gestured to an armchair and sat opposite to it. "May I be so bold to guess why you are here, sir?" The Queen asked with a slight smile. "I will guess you are here to ask me to get my cousin's family and the Luxlys out of Palace Nassau for a time.

And…possibly because you have something up your sleeve. Am I correct?" Johannes looked into the Queen's eyes, realizing how clever she was. "Yes, ma'am, you are correct."

"I must ask you if this is politically motivated, sir." the Queen's voice was slightly stern with this question. "Your Majesty, I feel that this is not only political, I feel it may be also related to the late Earl's position." Queen Wilhelmina looked away for a moment. "Do you feel others are in danger?" Johannes did not hesitate, "I am not sure, ma'am, and I cannot be sure until the family leave the palace for a short time."

The Queen turned back to face the Brigadier. "You are not sure at this point?" The tone in her voice was slightly sarcastic now. "I am almost positive, but I need to have the palace empty, or to appear empty to make sure, ma'am." Johannes almost felt ill with his response.

Queen Wilhelmina walked over to a bell pull and tugged. Less than a minute passed, and her secretary entered. "Sir, my secretary and I will construct a letter for you to take back to Earl Nassau. I require that you hand it to him directly the moment you return. Once my cousin reads it, I want you to have the Prime Minister telephone me. I will send word to him when you leave."

As the Queen sat at her desk, her secretary handed her the distinct blue paper and envelope. Johannes could see the Queen's crest embossed into the paper and the corner of the envelope. Queen Wilhelmina wrote out her instructions to Robert and looked up at Johannes. "I assume you know who committed these crimes." Johannes started to reply, but the Queen stopped him. "I only wanted to confirm, and your face gave you away, sir. Besides, you are the greatest detective our country has, after all."

The secretary folded the blue paper and slid it into the matching envelope. As he was handed the envelope, the Queen spoke softly. "I expect you to keep my family safe, and to make the arrest or arrests quickly. My family is very dear to me, sir. They are very dear to me indeed!" She finished the statement with a tone of urgency. "Meneer Michael is to turn seventeen next month, and I want it to be a happy event!" Johannes bowed and placed the blue envelope into his uniform pocket. "Thank you for your time, Your Majesty," and walked out of the grand room.

The secretary guided Johannes back to his motorcar. As he climbed into it, the secretary stopped him. "Her Majesty is anxious that you solve this quickly." Johannes turned to face the secretary and replied, "I expect it will be closed tomorrow evening." Johannes got into his motorcar and drove away.

The two-hour drive to Palace Nassau felt more like six to the Brigadier. He did not look forward to the Earl's reaction to the letter. Johannes has never been wrong, but he cannot afford to be wrong now. He could not help but think he would retire after he closes this case. Murder and kidnapping caused him to be more uncomfortable than any other types of crimes.

The lump in his throat returned as Johannes turned down the long drive to Palace Nassau. He could see several Rijkspolitie were stationed along the long drive. As the palace became visible, Johannes saw Bram standing at the side entrance. Bram opened the door for Johannes as he stopped his car. "Bram, do you know where His Lordship is?" Johannes asked with the lump now firmly in his throat. "Yes, sir, he and the families are in the anti-library." Bram offered to escort him, but the Brigadier waved him off.

Johannes walked up the main servants' stairs and down the long hallway. As he made it to the anti-library door, he could see Robert and James sitting with the boys at the far end. Robert noticed Johannes in his dress uniform, standing at the door. "James, please come with me." The Duke turned to see Johannes, and James followed Robert to the door.

"Brigadier, what is it?" Robert could see something in the Brigadier's face. Johannes had a look of apprehension. Saying nothing, Johannes pulled out the letter from Queen Wilhelmina. As he handed the blue envelope to Robert, Michael, and Charles had joined their fathers. "I see you have been to see my cousin," replied Robert to the sight of the blue envelope. "I have, sir." Johannes replied, "I am just returning from Apeldoorn now."

As Robert opened the envelope, the Prime Minister walked down the hall. "Did you know about this?" asked Robert as he held up the envelope. "I did, Robert, and I am to telephone Her Majesty now that you have it." As Robert and James read the letter, the Prime Minister telephoned the Queen. Johannes just stood and waited for Robert's reaction. Robert's face revealed nothing, yet Johannes knew Robert grew angry. Robert's body language became stiff, and he would not look at the Brigadier in the eyes.

As the Prime Minister replaced the telephone receiver, he stated, "Everything is set for your arrival tomorrow, and I am to join you." James could sense that Robert was growing angry about being told to leave his family home. "My dear friend, this means that the Brigadier is close to making an arrest," as he looked over to see the Brigadier nodding his head. Robert walked over to Johannes. "I am assuming you did not think I would leave if you asked me to." Robert's question was almost monotone with his anger. "That is correct, my lord. I cannot take the chance of you and the two families staying here while I set my trap. And, in order for my trap to be successful, the palace needs to be empty… or appear empty."

A sigh came from Robert as he turned away from Johannes. "Michael, please go get your mother and have her come here. Ask for your godmother to join us as well." Michael ran through the connecting door to his mother's study and returned quickly, with Mary and Elizabeth behind him. "We are all traveling to Het Loo in the morning," announced Robert with a tone of unhappiness. He continued, "The Knight Grand Cross has made arrangements with my cousin."

As the Brigadier departed, the Prime Minister approached Robert. "The staff will not be going to Het Loo. But they cannot remain here either." Robert returned to his chair and sank into it, the weight of the situation leaving him feeling defeated.

Chapter
18

Constable Henry Baker arrived and was being briefed by Major Dekker and Inspector Jansen. Johannes was on the telephone with someone he would not disclose to the others.

Brigadier de Groot was keeping things quiet and not releasing much information yet. The Koninklijke Marechaussee has issued the Constable a firearm.

As Johannes hung up the telephone, he wrote a quick note on a small piece of paper and folded it. Just as he finished, Lars knocked on the door. "Lars, please come close the door and come here," Johannes directed. Both Daan and Jan noted the tone in Johannes's voice.

Lars stepped into the small office and closed the door behind him as instructed. About fifteen minutes passed, a silent Lars walked out of the office and passed the Major, the Inspector, and Constable Baker. Daan stood up from his chair and walked towards Johannes.

Before he could speak, Johannes spoke with a tone that startled his three colleagues. "Close the door, sit down, and listen up!" Inspector Jansen knew at that moment his friend had solved this case. Constable Baker remained seated next to Jan, but visibly shaken by the Brigadier's tone. Daan quickly sat down after locking the door.

A visibly agitated Brigadier de Groot was pacing around the room, stroking his beard. "In an hour, Lars will summon all the London staff and the Nassau staff to the grand dining room on the ground floor. Lars will collect the four of us once everyone is ready."

Johannes chose the grand dining room because of the size. This was the only room that was large enough to accommodate both the London staff and Nassau staff away from listening ears. The double doors were wide enough to allow Daan, Jan, Johannes, and Constable Baker to enter side by side. But, it was only Johannes that entered the room completely. As he looked around the room, he noted all the staff. Everyone was there except one. He expected one of two people to be missing, and it was Emma that was missing. At the opposite side of the long table, Tess was sitting looking back at the Brigadier.

The Brigadier, in his black tailored three-piece suit, was impeccable. He stood straighter than even his friend Jan had seen him do. Inspector Jansen thought to himself, "He is the picture of Knight Grand Cross. He deserves the respect and gratitude from everyone." It was at this moment that he was the proudest to be not only a friend of Johannes but a colleague.

Johannes took four steps forward and placed his fingers on the surface of the mahogany table. His fingertips blanched as he pressed his weight onto them. Before he could even ask, Lars spoke up. "Emma did not report to work today because she is ill." Johannes did not take his eyes off of Tess as Lars spoke. Tess nodded in agreement with Lars and continued with, "She was up all evening with stomach issues, sir."

A now visibly angry Brigadier de Grote sat down in the chair and let out a sigh that caused Jan to stand next to his friend. Johannes looked up at Jan, but did not say a word.

Inspector Jansen knew at that moment they had another body, another murder. Jan placed his right hand on Johannes's shoulder and turned to a uniformed Rijkspolitie officer standing by the doors. With a sigh of his own, he announced, "Get a few officers and go to Emma's cottage." Looking back at Jan, he continued with, "Expect to find Emma's body either inside or near the cottage."

The Inspector's announcement drew a collective gasp from the staff, followed by a flurry of voices all asking the same questions at once. Johannes slammed his fist on the table, bringing instant silence. "Everyone in this room is innocent of the crimes that led to our being here," he said, his voice steady. "I know who killed the footman, who abducted Meneer Michael Nassau, and who murdered his lordship's secretary." Rising from his chair, Johannes fixed his gaze on Tess, leaning forward slightly. "I expected either you or Emma to be killed—but it could not be prevented."

Tess and the others stared in surprise. Johannes turned to Constable Baker. "I want you to put our plan into action." The constable gave a respectful bow. "Yes, my lord," he said, before turning and leaving the room. Only he and the Brigadier knew what that plan was. Major Dekker stepped closer to Johannes and Jan, voicing the question on everyone's mind. "You don't seem troubled by Emma's murder. What made you expect it?" Johannes didn't answer. Instead, he turned back to face the servants.

"The killer wants us distracted by this second murder. It was going to happen no matter what we did to stop it. He hopes this death will force an evacuation of House Nassau—and I'm happy to grant his wish. Each of you, along with the family, will leave House Nassau today."

The Brigadier looked to the London butler and gave a nod. George returned the gesture with a short bow, then left the room, snapping his fingers three times—a signal for the London staff to follow him out.

Lars took a step forward. "Ridder de Grote, may I begin what we discussed earlier?" Johannes nodded. As Lars left, he closed both of the grand dining room's large doors behind him. A clear click echoed as he turned the key in the lock. Johannes returned to his seat, taking several moments to study each of the servants who remained.

Tess remained seated at the far end of the room, now weeping softly and wiping tears from her face. Bram handed her his handkerchief. Both the Major and the

Inspector took their seats. Not a sound came from anyone—not even Tess. After several minutes, the staff door to the grand dining room opened, and Constable Baker stepped inside. Johannes gave him a nod, and the young man made his announcement. "Each of the servants will pack luggage for a week's travel. This includes Tess. You will be taken to London, where the Lord and Lady Nassau will provide accommodations.

An armed Rijkspolitie officer will escort each of you and remain with you as you pack. No questions will be answered, so please do not ask any." Tess was the last to stand up from the grand table. Johannes stood and said, "I want you to know that it was you or Emma. I know now that you are innocent, and I apologize. I hope you can accept my apology." Tess walked over to the Brigadier, who was standing at attention with an appearance of a Grand Knight. After shaking his hand, Tess walked down the servant's stairs to pack. Only Daan, Jan, and Johannes remained in the grand dining room.

As the three spoke quietly about the tasks ahead, a knock at the double doors interrupted them, followed by the sound of a key turning in the lock. Lars stepped inside and announced, "Major Dekker's men have secured House Nassau."

Several Rolls-Royce automobiles were lined up in front of Huis Nassau, ready to transport everyone to Het Loo Palace. The Koninklijke Marechaussee and Rijkspolitie had carefully planned the route, including alternative paths. Each Rolls would carry one plainclothes armed officer, while several more armed officers rode ahead and behind the caravan.

Lars reported to the old cook's quarters to meet Johannes. "I've ensured all the staff will be gone once the families have left," Lars announced. Johannes shook his hand gratefully. "Do you know when we can return to Huis Nassau?" Lars asked. Johannes replied, "I don't want anyone here for at least one week." Lars bowed and ascended the stairs to the first floor.

A large truck was carefully loaded with everyone's luggage, its cargo secured for the journey ahead. In the first Rolls-Royce, Robert, James, Michael, and Charles settled into the plush leather seats, their expressions a mix of anxiety and resolve. Riding with them was Willem, the plainclothes armed officer tasked with their protection, alert and watchful.

In the Rolls, Mary and Elizabeth sat quietly, exchanging occasional glances as they prepared for the trip. The final vehicle in the convoy carried the Prime Minister and the Minister of Defense, their presence underscoring the gravity of the situation as the caravan readied to depart.

All the ground-floor shutters had been firmly closed and secured, sealing the grand palace in near darkness. Johannes, Daan, and Jan stood together in the vast grand hall, their footsteps echoing softly as they methodically checked that every part of the plan was unfolding as intended.

The dim, shadowed corridors stretched out before them, the flickering remnants of fading daylight casting eerie patterns on the walls—an unsettling reminder of the house's weighty history. Meanwhile, Lars took extra precautions: he carefully gathered the keys from every member of the staff, each jangling softly in his hands, before locking them away in the heavy safe of his office. Just before he left, Lars turned to Johannes and handed over the master key ring.

Johannes, Daan, and Jan departed shortly after, leaving the Constable to remain inside, stationed below stairs. Once night fell, the three would return, relying on the Constable to let them in quietly through one of the staff doors. All the Rijkspolitie and Marechaussee personnel had left with their vehicles, the grand estate now eerily silent. The daily paper even carried a report announcing the family's trip to Het Loo, a visit to spend time with Her Majesty—an announcement meant to divert attention from the true circumstances.

Brigadier de Groot was taking a huge risk, hoping that leaving the palace empty would tempt someone to search it. Later, all three policemen met at Thijs' home in Delft. As Thijs served them coffee and poffertjes, Johannes explained his plan in great detail, using the maps drawn by Michael and Charles.

In the center of the map, the grand entry was marked with an "X" near the cloakroom. "This is where I want you to be, Major," Johannes explained as he points to the spot. He continued, "There's a small hole in the wall that looks out toward the doors of his lordship's study." Daan nodded, sliding his breakfast plate aside. Johannes tapped the map, pointing to two more "X" marks within the Earl's study. "There are two spots inside the study where we can wait," he said, looking toward Inspector Jansen. "I'll be here, and I want you here," he added, indicating their positions. "I've instructed Constable Baker to wait over here." Both Dekker and Jansen understood that the Constable's role was crucial—he was the only one still alive who could safely identify the killer.

Thijs cleared the table and brought fresh cups of coffee for the three officers. Just as he was about to leave, Johannes spoke up. "Thijs, what's the best route to get to Huis Nassau under cover of darkness?" Thijs studied the estate map carefully and pointed to the road leading to the estate church. "If I wanted to approach the property unnoticed, I'd park here and walk the rest of the way." He indicated a dirt path about two kilometers from the main road. Johannes turned the map around to examine the spot more closely. "Could you drive us here?" he asked, pointing to a place along the main road. Thijs glanced at the map and nodded in agreement.

The path from the main house to the church was heavily lined with trees, offering excellent cover. There were four roads leading to Huis Nassau from the main road, but this one was the most obscure—known only to those with a detailed map of the estate.

Daan leaned forward. "How do you think our killer will approach the estate, Johannes?" The three men studied the map silently, but it was Thijs who finally spoke up. "If I may, gentlemen?"

"Please," Jan replied. Thijs pointed to two main roads

that passed the front of the estate. "If I wanted to kill someone or steal something from a massive palace, I'd want to be close to my escape route. These two roads aren't good options." He then indicated another road. "This one goes past the barns and other outbuildings, but it also offers quick access out." Johannes's gaze flickered to that road — the same one near the barn where his best friend's body was found. Brigadier de Grote leaned back into his chair.

Jan could see something about his friend that made him realize exactly what was running through his mind. "Johannes, that makes sense, that is the barn where…" Jan did not finish his statement out of respect to Thijs. Johannes nodded. "It makes perfect sense. I bet that is where he will return tonight," replied Johannes. Thijs pulled up a chair to the table. "Is that where you found?" asked Thijs. Johannes looked up to Thijs to see the man who he saw as a strong but sentimental man who lost a best friend to murder staring directly at him. Johannes did not reply.

Thijs stood up and placed both of his hands on the table. "Gentlemen, I want one of you to explain to me how my best friend was killed and where you found him." Everyone's eyes were now focused on the Brigadier. Johannes knew he needed to explain in order for Thijs to have closure. "I will explain everything to you sir, but I need your word that you will allow us to handle the animal who killed your friend," exclaimed Johannes. Thijs agreed and sat down to the Brigadier's explanation.

After Thijs could hear the events that led to the

discovery of Antoon's body, his body relaxed. "Thank you, sir. I will promise to not do anything to jeopardize your plan. I will also agree to take the three of you to the estate. I just have one more request if I may." Johannes sat up and nodded. "I just ask that you let me know when you make the arrest," continued Thijs. Johannes agreed, and the three set off to prepare for their tasks.

In the summer months, sunset ranges from nine thirty to ten o'clock in the evening in the Netherlands. They waited until ten thirty to drive to the estate. Thijs will drive them to the agreed location and drive back to Delft. "I do not want to arrive too early nor too late. We should be inside Huis Nassau no later than eleven o'clock. Constable Baker has been instructed to let us into the palace's south servant entrance." Johannes continued, "The three of us will immediately arm ourselves and take our positions upon our arrival." Constable Baker was on time to let the three men into the palace.

Once inside, Baker explained to Johannes that the plan was in place and nothing to report at this time. "Gentlemen, the Brigadier has secretly kept eight Marechaussee in the attics. Each one is a sharpshooter from the military, and on different corners of the attics looking outside." Baker continued to explain that no one was seen coming onto the property. Each one took their positions and began the waiting game.

The clock chimed midnight, one o'clock, two o'clock, and then three o'clock.

Johannes thought their killer would not attempt

entering the palace after all. But the half hour chimed, and a dim light was seen under the library doors. This was the moment Dekker was ordered to not act until Johannes gave the signal.

Johannes, standing inside a large cabinet with lattice doors, could see the doors open to the library. He followed the light from a small torchlight up the bookcase, hiding the estate vault. He could see a silhouette of a large man but could not make out any other feature. The light became more and more focused on the bookcase the closer he got.

Daan remained in the cloak room, watching what he could see through the small hole in the wall. A pistol in his right hand started to shake slightly, but able to calm himself down quickly. Jan stood in the secret passage waiting for Johannes's signal to swing the door open. The secret passage was in arm's reach of the vault. The clicking of the combination dial clicked slowly.

There are three combination dials on the Nassau vault. Johannes could count, click-click-click, stop. "That's one," he thought. Click-click-click stop. "That's two." Click-click-click stop. Third and final for the first set of combinations. The second combination was counted the same way. Johannes could only see the dim light, but not what the killer was doing. He has not started the third. "What is happening?" he thought. He could hear a shuffle of paper, and then the killer started entering the third combination.

A loud "Click" followed by the sound of the vault handle turning echoed in the massive room. "NU!"

yelled Johannes as he jumped out of the cabinet and pointed his bright torch onto the killer and pointing his pistol. Jan swung the passage door open, blinding the killer, causing him to run towards the doors. Daan blocked his exit, causing him to run to the other side of the library. "STOP," yelled all three men as Constable Baker blocked the killer's exit from the side French windows.

The massive man, all in black, raised his hand that held a revolver. Johannes took aim and fired until the man fell to the floor, saving Constable Baker's life. The bullets from the killer's gun missed the Constable and shattered a large porcelain vase next to him. The gunfire and glass shattering deafened all the men in the room.

With their ears ringing, and the tunnel vision broken, all the police officials rushed to the killer's side. Johannes kicked the revolver to Jan and rolled the body over to his back. Constable Baker rushed over to see his face. "That is him, your lordship. I swear that is the man I know as Alexander Smyth." The constable held his torch onto the face of the man who killed the footman and attempted to kidnap Michael Nassau. Johannes fell to his knees next to the now-dead killer. "His real name is Alexi Smith, the brother of Emma Smith." Daan responded with "Jesus." Jan got closer to Johannes. "Was Emma her real name?" Johannes nodded, "Her position was legitimate. He used his sister's position in government to help collect information for his German party. I suspect that being a private secretary to Lord Nassau was pure luck." Constable Baker asked, "So the death of Emma proved to you that Alexander Smyth was actually Emma's brother?"

As Johannes stood up, he replied, "Correct, Baker, if Tess was killed, I would have been wrong. But having killed his own sister to shut her up proved to me who the killer was."

Commander Dekker picked up the telephone on the Earl's desk. After calling for backup and returning the receiver, he sat in the Earl's chair. "I am glad this is over, but I wish you all of my gratitude, Brigadier," exclaimed Dekker. Jan was now pulling the vault door open, "It was good that you had the vault emptied before tonight my friend." Johannes sat on the sofa facing one of the fireplaces.

A sigh came from him that sounded like a man who could catch his breath. "Now that this is over, I can explain something to each of you. Inside that vault were military plans, blueprints to a new aircraft, as well as names of our undercover military agents. The Prime Minister and the Earl were working on counterintelligence on the National Socialist German's Workers Party. We even have men from the Koninklijke Marechaussee undercover in the new party." Commander Dekker stood up and walked over to Johannes. As he placed his hand onto the detective's shoulder, he said, "You saved many lives tonight, apparently Brigadier." The large library clock chimed the hour.

After the last chime, vehicles could be heard approaching on the driveway. "I will go let them in," said Constable Baker. It was the Marechaussee and Rijkspolitie that Commander Dekker called.

Johannes walked over to the desk and sat in Robert's chair. "I have a telephone call to make, gentlemen. Would you mind if I make this alone?" Everyone walked out of the library, and Jan closed both doors. Alexi's body was still on the floor. Johannes kept his promise and telephoned Thijs.

After he explained everything to Thijs, he returned the receiver. Looking to his left, Alexi Smith was dead on the floor. The man was dead because of Johannes; however, he could not think about it like that. He could not question him, get all of his questions answered. What information did he pass off to the leader of his party?

At nine o'clock, Commander Dekker went down to the old cook's rooms to find Johannes sleeping in one of the armchairs. Normally, he would have let the man sleep, but he also knew that Johannes needed to be the one who telephoned Earl Nassau. The light taps of the shoulder woke up the sleep deprived Brigadier. "Brigadier, I think you should telephone Het Loo and notify the Earl Nassau that the nightmare is over." Johannes stood up and turned to face Dekker. "I request you make that telephone call. I am going upstairs to sleep for an unknown amount of time."

Johannes went to leave the now obsolete command center of the investigation. "Where are you going upstairs?" asked Dekker. Johannes just walked past him and climbed the servants' stairs to Antoon

Merten's rooms. Johannes climbed into the bed and quickly fell asleep.

Chapter
19

The House Nassau was once again filled with Rijkspolitie and Koninklijke Marechaussee, but this time, the air was lighter. The halls, once quiet with tension and grief, now echoed with laughter and music. Banners adorned with the Nassau crest lined the walls, and warm candlelight flickered in every corridor.

Today was a celebration: the shared birthday of Michael and Charles. Even Her Majesty Queen Wilhelmina was in attendance, mingling among the honored guests. There was only one notable absence — Robert. But he had an important duty: collecting the guests of honor.

Right at 5 o'clock, the train hissed to a stop at The Hague station. Robert stood tall on the platform, his posture straight and proud. As the doors opened, Brigadier Johannes de Groot stepped down first, followed by his wife. Both wore formal evening attire, dignified and elegant. Johannes bowed deeply to Robert.

"Today is not only for my son and godson," Robert said, beaming. "We want to celebrate you, Ridder de Groot." Robert offered no further explanation, only escorting the couple into the Royal Waiting Room of the station — a chamber few ever saw.

The room dazzled with opulence. Polished terrazzo floors stretched beneath heavy woven rugs, and rich red marble columns rose toward a gilded ceiling. Portraits of monarchs past lined the walls, their stern eyes silently watching. Beneath each portrait sat a silk-upholstered bench. It was a room that whispered legacy.

In the center stood the Prime Minister, dignified in a black tuxedo, holding a large blue envelope. As Johannes and his wife entered, the Prime Minister bowed. Robert stepped forward. "Not only did you solve a crime that haunted my ancestral house, but you protected my family and served this country with courage."

He handed the envelope to Johannes. "I hope what lies inside will tempt you."

Johannes hesitated, glancing at his wife. She gave him a gentle nod. "My lord," he said, "I already have a position."

"Just read," Robert replied, gesturing for him to sit. The envelope bore the official seal of Earl Nassau. As Johannes unfolded the letter, his eyes moved slowly down the page.

De hoogwelgeboren heer Johannes ridder de Groot,

the Earl Nassau requests you take the position of his private secretary and head of security...

Johannes's hand stilled. His wife let out a soft gasp.

You and your wife will be provided an estate cottage for life and a salary of 5,000 Guilders...

He read the offer again, stunned. A cottage on the estate for life, a substantial salary, a clothing allowance — far beyond what he ever imagined. The average salary for his rank was barely over 2,800 guilders. And now, a lifetime pension. He looked at his wife. Tears pooled in her eyes. Their small Amsterdam apartment, with its thin walls and noisy radiator, now seemed worlds away.

They sat in stunned silence until the door opened again. The First Chief Commissioner of the Rijkspolitie and the Commander of the Koninklijke Marechaussee entered with full dress uniform. Behind them were Inspector Jan Jansen and his wife. Jansen smiled knowingly. "I see you've read the letter." Johannes nodded. "I have."

"Do you know your answer?" He looked at his wife again, then at Robert, who waited quietly. Johannes rose, placed the letter back in the envelope, and approached Earl Nassau. He bowed. "My lord, it would be an honor and a privilege to serve your family and our country." Robert stood, relief and joy flashing across his face. Applause broke out in the room.

The First Chief Commissioner came forward, shaking Johannes's hand. "You've given so much to our service. But now, it is time to serve in a greater capacity."

Several black Rolls Royces transported the group to House Nassau. The streets they passed were lined with summer flowers, their fragrance wafting through the open windows. As they pulled into the estate, the silhouette of the palace glowed against the fading evening sky.

As Johannes stepped out, the gravity of his new role pressed gently on his shoulders. Before entering the grand hall, he paused at the portrait of Antoon.

Draped in a mourning band, the painting stood as a solemn reminder. Johannes reached up and gently adjusted the cloth. Pieter stood silently nearby, wearing his first tuxedo. He looked proud but still bore the softness of youth. He bowed respectfully. "Thank you, Ridder de Groot," he said, his voice steady. Johannes placed a firm hand on Pieter's shoulder. "Your father did not die in vain. He protected this family and this country. Take good care of your Oma." Pieter nodded, holding back emotion. Just then, Michael approached, followed by Charles, who—for once—looked neatly dressed and composed. "Sir, I didn't have time to thank you," Michael began. "Not before we went to Het Loo."

Johannes smiled warmly. "You do not need to thank me." Michael turned to Pieter. "He's not a servant anymore. He is my friend." It was a simple statement, but it struck deeply. The Nassau estate will provide for Pieter now, living in Gouda with his grandmother. He will be given an education, protected, and cherished— as his father would have wanted.

They led Johannes through the main hallway and into the large library, where the celebration was underway. The room shimmered with gold and green banners, crystal chandeliers, and a string quartet playing softly. As they entered, Michael cleared his throat.

"Your Majesty," he announced, "I present to you De hoogwelgeboren heer Johannes ridder de Groot." All eyes turned. Applause erupted. Johannes bowed deeply, but before he could rise, Queen Wilhelmina stepped forward. "It is I who should bow to you," she said, and she did. The room fell silent for a heartbeat, followed by everyone else bowing to the Knight Grand Cross.

As the party continued, Johannes stepped outside of the palace. The stars blinked softly above the gardens. Somewhere behind him, the Queen laughed, and children chased each other past the library door. Sounds and life that the palace had been missing.

He removed the Rijkspolitie credentials from his pocket—the same one he had carried through the darkest nights—and set it gently on the marble ledge beside him.

In the corner, a quartet played a soft waltz, the notes rising gently over the murmured conversations and clinking glasses. The footmen wore crisp uniforms in the Nassau livery—navy with gold braid—and moved gracefully through the crowd, offering crystal flutes of champagne and delicate hors d'oeuvres crafted in the royal kitchens. Countess Mary Nassau stood by one of the tall windows, her gown a soft lavender with silver embroidery that shimmered in the candlelight. She laughed quietly at something Queen Wilhelmina had said. Both women relaxed in a way that surprised many of the nobility in attendance.

It was rare to see a monarch speak so informally, so warmly — but tonight was different. Among the guests were high-ranking military officers, ambassadors from Belgium and France, and several members of the Dutch and British nobility. The Minister of Justice was engaged in conversation with a local mayor, and nearby, the Earl and Duke watched their sons have happiness that was absent for almost a month.

In a smaller drawing room off the main corridor, Pieter stood in a smart tuxedo, fidgeting slightly as he held a tray of poffertjes. He was not serving — but offering. It had been his idea to share some of his father's favorite foods with the guests, and the kitchen had worked carefully to replicate them exactly. He moved from group to group, offering them quietly, and accepting compliments with a polite nod. Michael, already tall for his age, stood beside Charles near the main fireplace, both boys under the watchful eye of Willem. Charles looked unusually composed tonight, his hair carefully parted and his jacket sitting just right on his small shoulders. Michael leaned over occasionally to whisper something to him, eliciting a stifled grin or nod. They seemed, at long last, happy again.

Behind the scenes, servants bustled with quiet efficiency, ensuring no glass went empty and no detail went overlooked. The air in House Nassau, once heavy with fears, now brimmed with renewal. The palace had not only survived tragedy—it had grown stronger because of it.

Upstairs, in Michael's room, a gift sat waiting—a delicate wooden box carved with the insignia of the House of Nassau. Inside was a watch, passed down by Robert's grandfather, now intended for Michael.

The hands were still ticking, their movement symbolic of something much deeper: legacy, endurance, and passaging burdens from one generation to the next. At seventeen years of age, Michael will now be known as Baron Nassau.

It is the 20th of July 1920. Michael and Charles' shared birthday. The two friends turned to Willem and nodded. It was their moment to take a gift to the Knight Grand Cross. With the help of their fathers, Michael and Charles could save two items to gift their hero.

Stepping out through some French doors, they met Johannes. Michael cleared his throat and Johannes turned. Michael stepped forward, pulling out the gift-wrapped wallet and piece of paper that helped Johannes solve the crime. Antoon's wallet and the piece of paper with Koninklijk Marechaussee written on it were not altered in any way.

Johannes stumbled, but quickly steadied himself. He did not take his eyes off the items and simply said, "Meneren, I...." but could not finish. At that moment, Jan and Daan joined them. Jan spoke up and finished his friends' thought. "Meneren, these items are the best gift the Knight Grand Cross could receive." The boys did a quick bow and returned to the party.

Author's Biography

Brandon Scranton was raised in Lincoln, Nebraska, where a deep-rooted sense of public service and a fascination with history helped shape his path as both a first responder and a writer. With over 29 years of experience as a Critical Care Paramedic, Brandon has served in a wide range of roles—from 911 metropolitan and county-based EMS to helicopter flight paramedicine and hospital-based critical care. He has also proudly served for 15 years as a Reserve and Part-Time Police Officer.

Brandon's lifelong interest in his Dutch and English heritage, paired with frequent travels to the Netherlands, inspired the creation of his debut novel, Secrets in the Shadows of House Nassau—a historical murder mystery set against the backdrop of a royal Dutch estate.

In September 2025, Brandon will be relocating permanently to the Netherlands, where he will continue writing and researching for the second installment in the series.